The Starvation Dybbuk:
A Cruel Tale of Love and Exorcism

By

BARAK A. BASSMAN

TELEMACHUS PRESS

THE STARVATION DYBBUK:
A CRUEL TALE OF LOVE AND EXORCISM

The publisher does not have any control over and does not assume any responsibility for author or third-party websites or their content.

Cover designed by Telemachus Press, LLC

Cover art: ©Copyright iStock Photo/1362265952/duncan1

Publishing services by Telemachus Press, LLC
7652 Sawmill Road
Suite 304
Dublin, Ohio 43016
http://www.telemachuspress.com

ISBN: 978-1-956867-65-7 (eBook)
ISBN: 978-1-956867-64-0 (Paperback)

Library of Congress Control Number: 2023910446

Version 2023.06.03

Table of Contents

The Starvation Dybbuk:
A Cruel Tale of Love and Exorcism

I. Hatred and Rage

REB YEHIEL WAS having a good day. The weather in the *shtetl* of W. was unusually warm for that time of year, and he managed to collect a couple of overdue business debts before the sinking sun on that Friday afternoon compelled him to go home to prepare for the *Shabbat* holiday. Later that evening, he prayed in the *bet midrash* with his fellow distinguished householders, the kind of learned men who enjoyed bantering a few words of Torah with each other.

After his prayers, the warm night beckoned, with its bright yellow moon and sparkling stars. As he took a leisurely stroll back to his house, the breeze brought lovely scents to his nose, although he was not sure what to call them—as a merchant who dealt in timber, he did not know much about flowers.

And when he entered the vestibule of his house, Yehiel saw another happy sight: His wife, Malke, stood before him in a lovely dress and shawl. Prowling around her feet were their twin sons, still too small to pray with their *tate*, but whom Malke had nevertheless dressed up in fine miniature black coats. While they smiled up at their father, they kept their fingers tightly wrapped around the folds of their mother's dress.

But where was his daughter Ruth? His eyes searched around the kitchen until they eventually found her sitting at the far end of the table. She was looking down and seemed upset. What could be troubling his Ruthele so? After all, it was *Shabbos* and they were about to eat—and he could already smell the warm delicacies waiting for his mouth.

But then Yehiel remembered: Ruth had bled for the first time, like a grown woman, only a few days ago. While he had not been there, Malke later told him that Ruth had been looking after her little brothers, when suddenly the blood started trickling down her leg. Her brothers screamed when they saw it, and then she screamed and ran off in tears. Malke followed her and then sat her down to explain how women manage such things. Yehiel had assumed that everything would be fine now: Ruth was becoming a woman, and she had a little scare, but her mother had taught what her to do.

Yet ever since that day, she walked about as if she had been judged guilty of some horrific crime and was now grimly submitting to her punishment. Or so Yehiel thought—but maybe he was wrong? Maybe this was just how girls were when this cycle of bleeding started?

It occurred to him that he had no idea how it would feel to just start gushing blood out of his body. Did it hurt? Was it sticky? Did it feel like urinating? But who urinates for days on end? Women were mysterious. How did the morning prayer put it? Blessed are you, Lord Our God, King of the Universe, Who has not made me a woman.

These musings reminded him that his Ruth was now thirteen years old, and she would soon be ready to marry and have children. He needed to meet with a matchmaker and start vetting possible bridegrooms and their families. Although before he did so, he had to figure out what he would offer as her dowry.

But not yet—he would not think any more about these matters until after the *Shabbat* holiday had ended. Yehiel sat down at the table, poured out cups of wine for himself and Malke, and recited the *kiddush*. When he was finished, they drained their cups and washed their hands.

Malke told Ruth to come help her serve the food that she had been cooking all afternoon. And what a wondrous delight that food was: roasted goose, *kreplach* filled with potatoes, golden *challah* loaves, and, best of all, fresh, warm honey cakes. Yehiel dug in like a glutton, as did the two little boys. Malke ate with a bit more restraint, but she smiled and laughed as she watched her men, both big and tiny, gobble down her cooking like starving beggars who had not eaten a decent meal for many weeks.

When Yehiel had eaten his fill, he slouched back in his chair, feeling merrily bloated. He beamed when he saw how the faces of his little boys were smeared all over with grease and crumbs. But then his eyes turned to his daughter Ruth sitting at the far end of the table. In front of her was a plate full of food, but she seemed to have touched none of it. Instead of eating, she was staring at some point down on the floor that Yehiel could not make out.

He called out to her: Ruthele, did you eat anything? You will feel better if you eat—nothing makes a heart bitter like hunger. Look, your mother has cooked up such delicacies that I doubt even King Solomon ate so well. He had a thousand wives you know, but not one of them could cook *kreplach* like your mother.

But Ruth said nothing in response.

Malke then chimed in: Ruth, answer your *tate* when he speaks to you.

Yet Ruth still did not speak or look up.

Yehiel tried again: Ruth, do you feel sick? Is there a pain in your stomach? Or in your throat? Maybe you can try to drink some chicken broth—Malke, don't you have some broth around here somewhere?

Ruth now looked up. When her eyes met his, Yehiel was startled to see that her gaze was so full of hatred. Then she picked up the plate in front of her and threw it against a wall, smashing it to pieces. Her little brothers screamed and ran to their mother.

Stunned by his daughter's crazy act, Yehiel shouted at her: Ruth, what is this? Your mother slaves away all afternoon in this kitchen so that we may show the Holy One, Blessed be He, the proper honor He is due on this holiday, and you throw her cooking at the wall like some drunken *goy* peasant brawling in a tavern?

And now Ruth finally spoke: You are disgusting, all of you! You say you want to honor *HaShem* but all you do is bury your faces in goose fat and wine. Watching you go at your food like filthy pigs, I can't bear it.

Ruth ran from the table. Yehiel heard her feet racing up the narrow staircase to the second floor, presumably towards her bedroom. He stood up to go follow her, but then Malke grabbed his arm. Let her be, she said. Girls her age sometimes get upset with their parents. It will pass.

And so, Yehiel sat back down and reached for another slice of honey cake. Although he was annoyed by Ruth's behavior—and also by the fact that he would now have to buy a new plate—he decided to follow Malke's advice. She understood girls and their moods; he did not.

Ruth did not emerge from her room for the rest of the night, even though her mother left heaping plates of food right outside her door and repeatedly pleaded with her to come out and eat.

Yehiel tried to distract himself from these troubles by studying his *Chumash* with Rashi's commentary, but he was unable to concentrate on the holy sage's explanations of the weekly Torah portion. Eventually, he put his book down and slipped out of the house to sit on the porch and enjoy more of the balmy night.

An hour or so later, when he went back inside, the house had become dark and quiet. He felt his way across the kitchen to the staircase and walked slowly up to his bedroom. There he found Malke fast asleep on her bed, snoring loudly. Yehiel sat on his bed opposite her and studied her face in the moonlight streaming in through the window. While there were some wrinkles around her lips and eyes, she was still quite pleasing. He had looked forward to lying with her that *Shabbos* eve and he was saddened that she had not stayed awake for him. He reasoned that she must have been too exhausted from Ruth's mad behavior.

And why did Ruth have to weary her mother and father? What was so terrible about enjoying *Shabbos* dinner? The Torah teaches us to choose life, and to choose life you have to choose to eat. And if you are going to choose to eat, why not eat fine food in honor of the holiday? Not to mention the *mitzvah* of giving honor to your mother for her labors in the kitchen preparing such a feast—a superb feast, a feast fit for a nobleman, or even a king. What was wrong with Ruth? Didn't she know that there were beggars sleeping on synagogue benches who could only dream of a freshly baked slice of honey cake?

Troubled by these thoughts, Yehiel tossed and turned in his bed for a long time. When he awoke the next morning, the sun was already risen, and he had to rush to dress and wash and get to the synagogue for morning prayers.

When he came back home, he found Malke in the kitchen sitting rigid and erect in a chair, staring silently ahead at the wall. She looked as if she was about to emit an extremely loud sigh. The little boys were yelling and fighting in a corner, but she paid them no mind.

Yehiel sat down next to her. Malke, he asked, what is the matter? And where is Ruth? Has she finally stopped her stupid pouting and eaten something?

Malke slowly turned her face towards him. He could not tell whether she wanted to burst out weeping or strike him with her fist, but it was clearly one or the other.

However, she remained silent.

After several more minutes elapsed, Yehiel pressed her again: *Nu*, what is all this sorrow and despair about?

This time, Malke responded, in a calm voice that trembled ever so slightly: Our Ruth has still not left her room. I have piled up an entire banquet outside her door and nevertheless she will not eat. But what can I do? She is stubborn.

Well, Yehiel asked, has she said anything? Maybe she is feeling ill?

Malke shook her head and sighed loudly. All she says, Malke replied, over and over again, is that this world of illusions is a prison for her soul. Food, she says, is like a pile of bricks pinning her soul to the ground. What is this *mishegas*? The world she has always lived in—this house, our kitchen, the town—these are all illusions now?

Malke's head then fell down into her palms and she moaned wretchedly.

Yehiel tried to reassure Malke that this was just some passing whim and soon enough Ruth would be pestering him to go to the matchmakers to find her a husband.

Malke smiled weakly in response. Yehiel was not sure if she believed him, but at least she did not argue.

Yehiel spent the afternoon sleeping—for one of life's true joys, in his estimation, was the lazy Saturday afternoon nap with a stuffed belly gently anchoring your *tuches* to the bed—and later paging through Rashi's commentary a bit more. While Ruth still did not come down and eat, he was able to put his crazy daughter out of his mind for the time being and get some rest.

Later that evening, Yehiel lit the *Havdalah* candle to bid farewell to the *Shabbat* holiday, and his mind turned to the week ahead. He would have to travel around the forests owned by the *Pan*, Count Czartoryski, to make sure the timber was being harvested and the logs sawed and sanded properly for transport upriver.

And he needed to figure out how he was going to set Ruth's dowry.

But before he could approach any matchmakers, Ruth needed to eat something to get the color back in her cheeks. A pale, trembling bag of bones would not appeal to a potential bridegroom.

And so, Yehiel turned to Malke and asked her to check on Ruth and see if she was ready to come down and eat. But Malke only groaned in response. Yehiel silently rebuked himself—he should have remembered that his wife had already worn herself out trying to beat some sense into the thick head of their *meshugenah* daughter.

Yehiel decided to go see for himself what was happening with their Ruth. Without saying another word, he got up from his chair in the kitchen and went upstairs. This time, Malke did not try to stop him. When he reached Ruth's door, he nearly tripped over the plates of untouched food piled up outside of it.

Yehiel knocked, but there was no answer. Pressing his ear against the door, he heard someone whispering. Was Ruth talking to herself? But no, it sounded like there were two voices—Ruth's voice and another, deeper voice, a man's voice. Could she be sinning with some man in her room? He thought he heard her make a gasping, moaning sound—what shame had she brought upon them?

Yehiel forced the door open and barged into her bedroom, ready to beat the scoundrel who had seduced his daughter. But when he looked around, he saw that Ruth was alone. Curled up in a corner on the floor, wearing a tattered housedress, she was staring at the ceiling and mumbling to herself, sometimes in her normal voice and sometimes in that other, deeper masculine voice.

Then Yehiel noticed that there were bruises and cuts all over the skin between her elbows and her wrists, with fresh blood dripping down from these wounds into her hands. And as Yehiel's eyes followed the flow of the rivulet of blood, he saw that in one of those hands his daughter held a small knife.

Yehiel lunged at her, grabbed the knife, and shook her hard. Ruthele, Ruthele, he cried, what are you doing? My Ruthele, my beautiful girl, how can you do this to yourself?

Ruth turned her head and looked at him—but with eyes that were glassy and dulled, like those of a corpse. Yehiel shuddered and grabbed her in his arms, hugged her and rocked her, and cried out for his daughter to please have mercy on him and wake up from her stupor—to forgive any sins he or Malke may have committed against her and just be his sweet girl again.

After a while, Ruth pulled away from him. Her eyes now glowed again with the light of life. Smiling and stroking his cheek, she said: *Tate*, don't be sad. I have seen a world filled with loveliness and purity, where there is no shame. I will leave here and go there. Someday, maybe, you will join me, you and *mame*. But for now, don't be sad. I have found a bridegroom and he will take me to his home in that land of loveliness and purity.

Yehiel could not make any sense of her words. Had she gone mad? But how does a normal, healthy Jewish girl suddenly lose her mind?

But before Yehiel could say something more, Malke abruptly entered the bedroom and pushed him aside. Holding a pile of cloth in one hand and a bucket of water in the other, she set about cleaning and bandaging Ruth's wounds. Ruth did not resist, and both women were silent, seemingly lost in their thoughts.

Yehiel quietly slunk away.

Ruth did not improve over the next few days. She would not eat; at most, she would let her mother pour some chicken broth down her throat. And she would not leave her bedroom, where she would lie staring at the ceiling or out the window, mumbling to herself. Occasionally Yehiel could make out a sentence here or there, but none of it made any sense.

Malke tried bringing Ruth's friends to her room, as she had always loved sitting and laughing with them. But Yehiel's heart sank when, after only fifteen minutes or so, he saw those same friends, with downcast eyes, silently shuffle out of the house.

He glanced over at Malke, but she turned away from him, buried her head in her hands, and sobbed. Even Malke, who could endure so many troubles without complaint, could not bear this. He reached over to comfort her, but she swatted his hand away.

Yehiel left his wife weeping on the porch and went back inside. The house was quiet. Malke had sent the little boys away to visit their aunt in the next town, where they could play with their cousins and be spared the sight of their sister suffering from this strange affliction. While Yehiel had agreed with the decision to send his sons away, he missed them now—he longed to hold little Menachem and Itzik in his arms and hug them and kiss their cheeks.

After standing alone in the silent kitchen for a long time, Yehiel went upstairs. It had been a couple of days since he had last seen Ruth. Malke had insisted that she knew best how to take care of their daughter—after all, what could Yehiel know? He was a man, and he had never endured the sadness and longing than can eat away at a young girl's heart.

But now Yehiel missed his Ruth too. And maybe he could do something? He was her father, and he did know some things about the world. When his Ukrainian foreman, who led his logging crews in the forest, had been sick two winters ago, Yehiel had been the one to fetch the doctor and arrange for his care. Maybe Yehiel knew more about helping the sick than Malke realized?

Yet when Yehiel entered Ruth's room, he saw a ghastly sight. She was horribly pale, and the bones in her wrists poked through the skin like jagged rocks. She was lying on her bed, eyes wide open, smiling and cackling and mumbling at the ceiling. Wearing a torn dress that exposed her flesh in an indecent manner, she was digging her sharp fingernails into her breasts and tearing at her skin until it bled.

She did not look at her father or acknowledge his presence in any way.

After initially hesitating about what to do, Yehiel walked over to the bed, pulled a blanket over her torn clothes, and moved her hands away from the bleeding sores on her skin. Sitting down next to his daughter and cradling her head in his arms, he felt tears well up in his eyes.

Ruthele, my Ruthele, he said, why are you afflicting yourself this way? Every day should not be *Yom Kippur*—and even on *Yom Kippur*, we do not tear our skin to shreds. Ruthele, don't you want to be happy again? To stand one day under the *chuppah*, with your *mame* and *tate* at your side, and wed your bridegroom? To feed a baby at your breast, your baby, with its big eyes looking up at you?

Twisting her head slightly, Ruth looked up at her father, raised her neck, and stretched her mouth toward him. Yehiel thought that perhaps she wished to say something, and so he lowered his ear towards her.

But then she spit in his face.

Yehiel screamed and jumped up. Ruth pointed her finger at him and laughed, in a voice that sounded strangely deep for a thirteen-year-old girl.

Yehiel stormed out of Ruth's room. Unable to bear this madness any longer, he gathered some clothes, a prayer book, and food, and hitched his horse to his wagon. He told Malke that he needed to spend a few days in the forest, checking on the progress of his work crews in cutting down the *Pan*'s trees and sawing the trunks into logs.

In response, Malke nodded absently and did not try to detain him.

As Yehiel departed from the *shtetl* and entered the forest road, he felt his heart lighten and he breathed more easily in the crisp air. He remembered back to the moment when he had first seen his Ruth as a newborn baby. The midwife had brought him to see his wife and new daughter in the morning after the birth. Tiny Ruth was tightly swaddled in a colorful, striped blanket. When the midwife handed him the baby to hold for the first time, he had been terrified—what if his fingers slipped? She was so fragile and small.

He rocked her in his arms. She jerked her arm until it got loose from the swaddling and stuck out like a tree branch from the tight bundle. He put his finger into her palm, and she closed her tiny soft hand around it. He had never felt such joy as he did in that moment when his baby daughter held onto him with all her little strength. She seemed determined to never leave her *tate*.

Another memory came to Yehiel. Ruth was three or four years old. He had been away for a few days, traveling through the forests with the *Pan*, who was inspecting the timber business on his estate and reviewing his accounts. Yehiel was sorely tired when he returned home again.

Right after he entered the door of his house, little Ruth ran up to him and grabbed his leg so firmly that he could not move. Yehiel reached down and picked her up and held her close to his face. She grabbed his cheeks and kissed his forehead. And then she said in a stern tone: *Tate*, no more going away like that. You stay right here from now on. No more forests and no more *Pan*. You stay right here and we will make tea together.

Yehiel sighed as he remembered these happy moments, which seemed so distant that they might have come to pass in the days when the Temple still stood in Jerusalem. Lord of the Universe, he said to himself, what has happened to my Ruthele? What has my beautiful daughter ever done to merit such suffering?

II. The Search for a Cure

YEHIEL SPENT THREE days in the forest, putting Ruth and Malke and his domestic troubles out of his mind. He spoke to his foreman and his work crews, and he supervised their cutting and sanding and loading the logs onto wagons for transport to the river boats. At night, he drank himself into oblivion with the foreman, who had luckily brought several bottles of good vodka into the woods with him. By the time Yehiel returned home he was in good spirits.

But when he walked through the door of his house again, the first thing he saw was a fat peasant woman in a red kerchief storm off as Malke screamed wild curses down upon her head. Who was that? he asked his wife. And what just happened?

After collapsing onto a chair and groaning loudly, Malke then told him that, out of desperation over Ruth's condition—which had still not improved, only worsened—she had visited a Ukrainian wise woman who lived in a hut just beyond the town. This woman had promised a cure in exchange for twenty-five zlotys. Once Malke had paid her, she came to their house and locked herself inside Ruth's bedroom. With Malke listening at the door, she intoned various incantations and seemed to be burning herbs whose rancid stink leaked out through the keyhole.

Ruth, however, only laughed at the peasant woman.

This went on for hours.

Malke fell asleep on the floor in the hallway outside her daughter's bedroom.

She awoke to the sound of a loud thud. Unsure what had happened, she knocked on Ruth's door. When there was no response, Malke forced her way inside. And there she saw the so-called wise woman lying on the floor, covered in vomit, and trembling. Ruth meanwhile was sitting on her bed and staring peacefully out the window.

Malke was furious. What kind of a cure was this? The so-called wise woman was a liar and a thief. And so, she went back into the hallway, grabbed a broom, and beat the peasant with it until she stood up and ran away.

When Malke finished her tale, she spit three times onto the ground.

Yehiel told his wife that she had been a fool to put her trust in some ignorant peasant witch. As Ruth's condition had clearly not improved, he promised to fetch the doctor—the real doctor, the one who tended to the families of rich merchants and even to the *Pan* himself in his great manor house. This doctor was a learned man, Yehiel said, and he would know how to heal Ruth.

And so, the next day, shortly after lunch, the esteemed doctor—a graduate of some famous Gentile university somewhere, Krakow or Konigsberg or the like, Yehiel could not recall exactly—came to their house. Yehiel led the doctor upstairs to Ruth's bedroom and lingered in the doorway as he examined the patient. While Ruth mutely complied with the doctor's instructions and let him prod and poke and look and listen wherever he desired, her eyes were full of contempt and at a few points she all too obviously stifled her laughter.

When Ruth undressed for the doctor, Yehiel was shocked to see how many bruises and lesions there were all over her arms and chest. They looked like the claw marks of a wild, rabid cat—had she actually scratched herself so viciously? Was she trying to tear her skin off?

And she had become so thin that Yehiel could see her bones and ribs pushing out through the flimsy covering of bruised and cut skin.

Once he was finished with his examination, the doctor asked to speak with Yehiel privately. Ruth did not protest or even seem to care in the slightest about what the doctor might have to say. To the contrary, she let out the kind of loud sigh that a person makes when they have been too patient with a fool and went back to sitting on her bed and staring out the window.

Yehiel led the doctor back downstairs to the kitchen, where Malke was waiting for them. Well, Yehiel asked, what is the matter with my Ruth? And how do we get her well again?

The doctor sat down at the kitchen table and looked at his hands. He seemed to be composing his thoughts carefully. After a few moments of silence, he spoke: Yehiel, my friend, there is nothing wrong with your daughter's body except that she has not taken nourishment in far too many days and she is scratching away at her skin. Any physical malady can be readily cured with a brisket and a few bandages. But you already knew that your daughter needed to eat again. I am afraid that her true sickness, whatever it is that prevents her from eating again like a healthy young woman should, is of a spiritual nature and beyond the ken of medical science. My sincere apologies, but I can be of no further assistance. Under the circumstances, I will waive my customary fee.

And with that, the esteemed doctor stood up and left.

Now it was Malke's turn to scold Yehiel: So that was your esteemed doctor? Went to the famous university so that he could tell us that a girl who is starving herself needs to eat? Your esteemed doctor is every inch the idiot as my wise woman from the hut. May they all fall down a well.

Yehiel sighed. He had been sure that the doctor was going to diagnose Ruth's illness and lay out the treatment regimen to bring her back to health. So, what to do now? There was nothing wrong with her body. Yet for some bizarre reason, she was starving and scratching herself and would not listen to her mother or her father or anyone else. Maybe he should send for another doctor, a better one? But who would that be? Their *shtetl* was many miles from the nearest large city. Ruth was in no shape to travel and would probably refuse to get in the carriage anyway. To send for a doctor from a faraway city to come to him would cost a fortune—if he could even afford it—and take weeks, maybe months, to arrange. Meanwhile, his Ruth was living on a few drops of broth a day. How long could she last? Would she be gone from this world by the time the doctor could reach her?

And would another doctor say anything different? After all, these famous doctors all trained at the same universities with the same books and the same teachers. The doctor who had examined Ruth was perfectly competent in his science. If it got him nowhere, then maybe this was a spiritual malady.

Yehiel now stood up from the kitchen table and said to Malke that he was going to consult with the town's rabbi. If she was suffering from a spiritual malady, then maybe Ruth simply needed to hear some words of Torah to comfort her soul.

Although it was rainy and cold outside, Yehiel ignored the bad weather and walked quickly toward the rabbi's house. But when he reached the building and saw the steps leading up to the porch, he suddenly panicked and fled to the *bet midrash*. Once there, he grabbed the first book that his fingers touched, sat down alone on a bench in a far corner, opened to a page at random, and pretended to study.

But he could not focus on the text in front of him. Instead, he thought: Why did I tremble before the threshold of our town's rabbi? I have known this man for many years. He is honest, pious, and a distinguished scholar. And yet . . . what would he say about Ruth? Word had no doubt spread about the town that Ruth was ill, but Jews get ill all the time. Yet this was no fever or cough. No, she had simply decided out of nowhere one night to stop eating and to start tearing her skin to pieces. What could be the explanation other than that Ruth was a madwoman? And what sane father would ever let his son marry a madwoman?

If Yehiel told the truth of this matter to the rabbi, then wouldn't he naturally tell his wife? After all, what did an old man with his nose buried in the Talmud know about the afflictions and sorrows of a thirteen-year-old girl? Of course, he would seek her counsel. And once she knew, she would tell someone else—that is how women are, they don't mean to be cruel, but they like to talk with each other, to be friendly, and so things slip out of their tongues without them meaning for it to happen. And once one knows, they will all know. And then the matchmakers will know. There won't be a dowry big enough to secure his Ruthele a decent husband. No, he will be forced to pay through the nose for some ignorant lout son of a blacksmith, or worse. And what kind of a life would that be for Ruth, tethered to such a wretched husband? To have an illiterate imbecile as a father to her children?

But on the other hand, what choice did he have? What kind of a father would let his daughter starve herself to death? Was his heart made of stone? He had to do what he could do. If the doctors and the wise women were of no use, then he had to try the rabbi. Someone, somewhere, must know how to end Ruth's suffering.

And so, Yehiel stood up again, put the book away on its shelf, and left the *bet midrash* to walk back to the rabbi's house. This time, with his heart pounding, he mounted the steps and knocked at the door.

After a brief but agonizing silence, the rabbi's wife came to the door. Reb Yehiel, what a wonderful surprise, she said. Please come in.

Yehiel followed her inside to a parlor room, where he sat down on an upholstered red chair and took the glass of brandy that she handed to him. A crackling fire spread its warmth and cast a soothing, soft orange light.

Meanwhile, the rabbi's wife had gone off to find her husband.

About a quarter of an hour later the town's rabbi joined Yehiel. He asked: What has brought you here for this unexpected visit—is something wrong, Heaven forbid?

Yehiel sighed and put down his glass. He reminded himself again to speak forthrightly—that this was a matter of life and death for his Ruth. And so, Yehiel told the rabbi everything that had happened: how Ruth had stopped eating; how she had mortified her flesh; her crazy moods; and how even the doctor—the good one who had studied at the famous Gentile university somewhere—had despaired of being able to help her. Yehiel decided not to mention that his wife had turned to some Ukrainian peasant witch—the rabbi did not really need to know *that* detail.

When Yehiel finished, he felt the tears running down his cheeks and his hands were shaking.

The rabbi responded gravely that this matter was clearly quite serious, and Ruth's life might well hang in the balance. He said he needed to finish a letter he was writing—he was almost done; it would just take a minute—and then they would go together to see her.

After the rabbi left the room, Yehiel reached for the glass of brandy and drained the rest of it down. But the drink did not steady his nerves. He hoped the rabbi could do something to help her, perhaps reason with her somehow or maybe know the right prayers to drive away her affliction. But what if he could not? Would Yehiel be forced to watch his Ruth wither away? He saw in his mind again how Ruth had appeared when the doctor examined her: deathly pale, bones jutting sharply out of her ribcage, and scratch marks and bruises and black scaly scabs all over her skin. What sin had he ever committed to merit a daughter who would do this to herself? After all, Ruth could not be suffering for *her* sins—for what horrible sin could a thirteen-year-old girl have possibly committed in her brief life?

By now sobbing uncontrollably, Yehiel fell to the floor and writhed about like a wounded animal. The flood of tears blinded his eyes and clogged his nose, and he gasped and wheezed for breath.

Yehiel did not realize that the rabbi had returned until he felt a firm hand grab his face and apply a soft handkerchief to clean him up. After he had helped Yehiel back to his feet, the rabbi said: Reb Yehiel, my friend, your Ruth needs your strength, not your tears. Let us go to her now.

Yehiel nodded and silently led the rabbi back to his house. He knew the rabbi's counsel was wise and that he needed to be strong. He quietly begged the Holy One, Blessed be He, to give him that strength.

When they arrived at Yehiel's house, they briefly greeted Malke and then went up the staircase to Ruth's bedroom. They found her lying on her bed staring up at the ceiling. Her dress was twisted and wrinkled and stained with blood from her many sores.

The rabbi sat down on the bed next to her, while Yehiel remained standing in the doorway. The rabbi gently asked Ruth how she was feeling. He said that her parents were concerned that she was not eating enough. The Torah teaches that we must choose life. The Holy One, Blessed be He, wishes that all of Israel's daughters will grow up to be happy wives and mothers, blessing the candles on *Erev Shabbos* and comforting their crying babies during the night.

Ruth turned her head towards the rabbi and coldly stared straight into his eyes. And then she said: Liar! Idiot! You do not understand what the Holy One, Blessed be He, truly desires. You are a slave to this lowly material world—you are a slave to your fat, bouncing belly.

The rabbi sighed and shook his head. Closing his eyes and swaying slightly, he began to recite a prayer for the healing of the sick.

In response, Ruth grabbed the rabbi's beard and tore off a patch of hair.

The rabbi stopped his prayer.

And then a voice which was not Ruth's, a deeper masculine voice, burst forth from her lips and railed at the rabbi in a language that was not Yiddish. At first, it sounded to Yehiel like Hebrew, but it was not Hebrew. And then he realized what it was: Ruth was speaking in Aramaic, the language of the *Gemara*, which he recognized from his own past studies of the Talmud. But how could Ruth know Aramaic? As she was a girl, Yehiel had never sent Ruth to *cheder*, much less to a *yeshiva*. So where could she have learned Aramaic? And more than merely learned—she was as fluent as the holy sage Abaye of blessed memory, may his merit protect us.

The rabbi also looked startled. He said something back to Ruth in Aramaic but spoke so quickly that Yehiel could not make out the words. Then Ruth's new masculine voice replied with a torrent of curses and abuse in Aramaic, insulting the rabbi's intelligence and accusing him of all sorts of sins, from eating *treyf* food to adultery with his Gentile maid to smoking a pipe on *Shabbos*.

But this time the rabbi did not bother responding to her. Instead, he stood up, walked over to Yehiel, motioned for him to leave, and then gently closed the door to Ruth's bedroom behind them. Yehiel followed the rabbi back downstairs into the kitchen, where they rejoined Malke.

Malke looked at them and said: *Nu*, have you figured out what is wrong with Ruth?

The rabbi sighed. He said that he feared Ruth might be possessed by an evil wandering spirit, a *dybbuk*. The voice that had spoken from her lips was not that of a young girl, and no Jewish maiden could speak Aramaic like that. The matter was beyond his skill and knowledge. They needed a scholar learned in the practical *Kabbalah*, someone who knew how to wield combinations of secret holy names to expel spirits. Fortunately, there was such a man not too far away—Rabbi Israel ben Eliezer, the Baal Shem Tov. This Israel Baal Shem was renowned for his prowess against the forces of the *sitra achra*, demons and wandering spirits and all the rest. The rabbi promised to send a messenger to fetch the Baal Shem Tov that very night.

III. The Exorcism

YEHIEL WENT TO sleep that night feeling lighter and happier than he had for some time. He reflected: If Ruth was possessed by a *dybbuk*, an evil spirit, then the torments she was suffering were on account of the many sins committed by that spirit when it once walked the Earth in the body of a man. The rabbi would summon this Baal Shem Tov, and he would expel the *dybbuk*. And then all would be good again.

The following day, Yehiel waited anxiously for the Baal Shem Tov to come to his *shtetl*. To soothe his nerves, he sat in the synagogue reciting Psalms for Ruth's recovery. As the sun was setting and the pink light of dusk shone through the synagogue windows, a loud commotion outside broke Yehiel's concentration. Before he could gather his wits about him again, the synagogue doors burst open and the town rabbi led a huge crowd right up to him.

Standing next to the rabbi was a short Jew with a thick beard and a wrinkled gabardine smeared with what looked like chicken fat. The rabbi introduced this slightly disheveled man as Rabbi Israel ben Eliezer, the Baal Shem Tov, who had immediately traveled to their town upon hearing the news of Ruth's possession by an evil spirit.

The Baal Shem Tov said to the rabbi: Is this the father?

And the rabbi said yes.

Then the Baal Shem Tov spoke to Yehiel: I see you have been praying for your daughter's recovery. That is good. Your prayers will help gather the angels necessary for the struggle against the *dybbuk*. Take me now to your daughter. I must examine her first, and then we can prepare what is necessary.

Eager to start the fight against the *dybbuk* and free his daughter, Yehiel quickly led the Baal Shem Tov, the rabbi, and several of the Baal Shem Tov's disciples from the synagogue to his house. They strode hurriedly through the kitchen, past a startled and bewildered Malke, up the stairs to Ruth's bedroom.

They found Ruth lying on her bed, with her face turned to the wall, her gaze glassy and distant. The Baal Shem Tov approached her side, recited a blessing, and loudly praised the beauty of the setting sun and how the Holy One, Blessed be He, had created such a lovely world for His people Israel.

But Ruth snapped back that this world was filthy and vile.

The Baal Shem Tov replied: And is this the reason why you refuse to eat? For that is what I was told—that one day, a healthy young girl, ready to become a Jewish bride, suddenly will not eat. *Nu?*

This time Ruth did not respond.

Then the Baal Shem Tov spoke again: Turn over and show your face to me.

But Ruth curled into a tight ball and hid her face in her chest.

The Baal Shem Tov reached out with his hand and held it over Ruth's body. Then he rapidly recited a wild barrage of words that sounded vaguely like Hebrew to Yehiel, but which were like no Hebrew expressions he had ever heard before.

Ruth screamed and begged him to stop. Malke ran into the room and lunged for the Baal Shem Tov, but one of his disciples intercepted her and threw her to the ground. She retreated to Yehiel standing in the doorway and implored him in a whisper to do something—couldn't he see that their Ruth was suffering?

But Yehiel replied: What could he do? She had been suffering long before the Baal Shem Tov came. And at least maybe he could expel whatever evil spirit had possessed her.

Malke looked as if she were about to say something in protest, but then quietly shuffled back downstairs.

A couple of minutes later, the Baal Shem Tov abruptly stopped reciting his bizarre babble of Hebrew-like words. Ruth now uncurled her body and sat up in the bed.

The Baal Shem Tov now peered intently into her eyes, as if he were searching for a valuable item that had fallen down inside her pupils.

After a while, the Baal Shem Tov backed away slightly and said: *Dybbuk*, I can see you inside this girl. You are inflicting terrible agonies upon her—and you are thereby accumulating even more sins for which the Heavenly Tribunal and the Avenging Angels will hold you to account. Tell me, will you leave her now, of your own will? If you leave her now, I have the promise of the rabbi of this town that two men will pray each day for your soul and study a page of Talmud each morning in your honor. Regardless of what sins you may have committed in your prior incarnation as a man, their prayers and study will shield your soul from angels and demons who would do you harm. Will you leave her body now, exiting through her little toe?

But Ruth hissed and foamed at the mouth and shouted, in her own voice, that the spirit inside her body was her true bridegroom and she did not want him to leave.

The Baal Shem Tov did not reply but instead gave a signal to his disciples. They pounced upon her, withdrew several ropes from a bag they had been holding, and bound her hands and feet so tightly that she could hardly move.

Ruth did not resist them, but merely laughed and spit in their faces.

The Baal Shem Tov ordered two of his disciples to remain with Ruth. He gave strict instructions that they were not to speak with her or loosen her bonds. Rather, they must each don their *tallis* and *tfillin* and recite Psalms for the redemption of the girl's tortured soul. The Baal Shem Tov then instructed Yehiel and the other disciples to depart from Ruth for the time being.

Back downstairs in the kitchen, the Baal Shem Tov told Yehiel and Malke to leave the house for the night and take their other children with them. He and his disciples would prepare for the exorcism ritual, which would be performed the next day in the synagogue.

Malke went with their little sons to a nearby relative's house. As Yehiel told his wife that he wished to spend the evening in solitary prayer, they had agreed to part for the night. He walked alone in the cold night, wandering into the forest for a while. There, amidst the screeches of the owls, he felt his nerves calm.

But then Yehiel's belly twisted with hunger, and he went back into town to the local inn, where the innkeeper served him bread and onions and pickled herring. Yehiel started to explain to the innkeeper that he could not sleep in his home that night, owing to –

But the innkeeper cut him off: Reb Yehiel, the whole town knows of your suffering. We are all praying for your Ruth tonight, and we will be there tomorrow in the synagogue to help cast out the *dybbuk*. You can stay here tonight. I will make up a room—no charge. Gather your strength for tomorrow's great trial.

Lying alone in his bed in the inn later that night, Yehiel's thoughts were full of worry. While he was relieved that someone at last was coming to Ruth's aid, did she need to be brought into the synagogue so the entire town could watch her writhe about in her misery? Would this humiliation ever be forgotten? And now there was no chance he could hide what was happening from a possible bridegroom. What if the bridegroom and his family worried that Ruth had committed some sin that allowed the *dybbuk* to penetrate into her? Would they still trust that she was a righteous daughter of Israel?

But on the other hand, what else could he do? If the Baal Shem Tov, a scholar deeply learned in practical *Kabbalah* and esoteric wisdom, said that this was the way and such-and-such must be done, who was he to argue? After all, when it came to wandering spirits, Yehiel was an ignoramus, a boor, an *am ha'aretz*.

The innkeeper roused Yehiel early the next morning and told him to hurry up, as the Baal Shem Tov was already leading special morning prayers to prepare for the battle with the *dybbuk*. So, Yehiel dressed and washed quickly and in the blink of an eye found himself in a synagogue so densely packed that there was not an empty bench to sit on. However, when he looked up to the women's section in the balcony, he did not see anyone there, so at least Malke would be spared the shame of watching her daughter be paraded before every householder in the *shtetl*.

The Baal Shem Tov called out to Yehiel to come forward and sit in the front of the synagogue, next to the town's rabbi. The Baal Shem Tov and his disciples were all dressed in long white robes, with prayer shawls on their shoulders and *tfillin* wrapped around their arms and foreheads.

After Yehiel took his place, the Baal Shem Tov ordered the Jews assembled there to recite Psalms for Ruth's soul. As Yehiel mechanically rattled off the Psalms he knew from memory, he watched the Baal Shem Tov standing on the *bimah* in front of the lectern from which the weekly Torah portion was read. Yehiel could not make out what the kabbalist was saying in his prayers, but his lips moved rapidly and his body rocked gently.

Then the Baal Shem Tov closed his eyes tightly and swayed with great fervor.

A few minutes later, he suddenly fell down from the *bimah* onto the floor in front of Yehiel. His mouth foamed, his limbs shook, and his eyes opened wide, revealing two completely milk white orbs.

Eventually, he stood back up, wiped the saliva from his face with his sleeve, and ordered one of his disciples to go fetch the possessed girl, as he was ready now to do battle with the spirit. He instructed the Jewish householders to continue with their Psalms until Ruth arrived.

About half an hour later the *shammes* directed the Jews inside the synagogue to move aside to make a corridor. Once the path was cleared, the disciples of the Baal Shem Tov carried Ruth's bed, with her bound tightly on top of it, into the synagogue and placed it down upon the *bimah* before the Baal Shem Tov. While she was wearing the same tattered housedress, at least, Yehiel thought, it seemed to cover her enough to preserve her modesty, *baruch HaShem*.

Cries of lamentation greeted Ruth's entrance, but she seemed not to care. Yehiel called out to her as she passed, but she did not respond or even look in his direction. He burst into tears, even though he tried to stop himself from making such a shameful display. The town's rabbi put his hand on Yehiel's shoulder, which steadied and comforted him.

The bed with Ruth on top of it was placed down in front of the lectern on the *bimah*, so all the assembled Jewish householders could easily watch what was going to happen. The Baal Shem Tov ordered the *shammes* of the synagogue to take out seven *shofroth* and hand them to his disciples. Then another set of disciples went to the ark at the back of the *bimah* and removed seven Torah scrolls. Finally, the *shammes* lit seven black candles and placed them in a semi-circle around Ruth's bed.

After ordering the congregation to be silent, the Baal Shem Tov gave a signal to his disciples, who then simultaneously blew three tremendous blasts from the seven *shofroth*—a deafening roar that made Yehiel grab his ears and double over in pain.

When the *shofar* blowing had finished, the Baal Shem Tov addressed Ruth's body:

Dybbuk, foul spirit, reveal your name and confess the sins for which you are cursed to wander the Earth without rest.

But the *dybbuk* did not answer.

The Baal Shem Tov waved his arm at two more of his disciples, who rose and approached Ruth's body lying on the bed. One of them carried a bowl filled with a brownish powder, while the other held a lit candle in his hand. The disciple with the candle dipped the flame into the powder, and a pillar of dusty smoke shot up into the air. The disciple holding the bowl pushed the fumes right under Ruth's nostrils, so the smoke burned straight into them.

A masculine voice coming out of Ruth's mouth screamed in agony. Everyone sitting near the *bimah*, including Yehiel, coughed violently from the scorching, putrid fumes. Yehiel was scared that the Baal Shem Tov's disciples were going to hurt his daughter, and he rose to stop them, but the town's rabbi grabbed his shoulder and pulled him back down.

He whispered to Yehiel: Do not interfere, for there is no other way.

Yehiel reluctantly sat down again.

After a few minutes, the disciples put out the fire in the bowl and stepped away from the bed. Then the Baal Shem Tov repeated his demand that the *dybbuk* state its name and confess its crimes.

This time the *dybbuk* hissed and spat at the Baal Shem Tov. Ruth's body writhed miserably, but the tightly knotted ropes held it securely in place.

The Baal Shem Tov closed his eyes and began to sway back and forth. He extended his right forefinger towards Ruth and rapidly recited a string of what sounded to Yehiel like nonsense words in Hebrew. But the town's rabbi whispered to him that these were combinations of hidden, true names of powerful angels.

The *dybbuk* let out another scream. Ruth's eyes bulged and her body flinched this way and that, as if she were dodging vicious blows from an invisible attacker.

Speaking through Ruth's mouth but in a deep masculine voice that was not hers, the *dybbuk* said, in a trembling tone: Send them away, please, send them away from me. I see their whips of fire and I hear their curses raining down upon me.

The Baal Shem Tov replied: If you wish for me to send the avenging angels away, then promise to tell me your name, *dybbuk*, and confess your crimes and reveal why you have possessed the body of this innocent daughter of Israel.

The *dybbuk* hastily promised to reveal whatever the holy *tzaddik* asked him to reveal.

The Baal Shem Tov nodded, closed his eyes, and once more uttered a long series of unintelligible Hebrew-sounding words. After he was finished and had opened his eyes again, the *dybbuk* began to speak in a calm, measured voice. Yehiel leaned in close to listen. This is what he heard the spirit say:

My name is Chaim, son of Mayer, the wine merchant. As a boy, I did nothing but study. I learned whole tractates of the Talmud by heart. Yet I eventually tired of the surface meanings of the Torah. I discovered the works of the *Kabbalah*, books that revealed the esoteric secrets, and I devoured them day and night. I ignored all other matters—I lived only for my love of contemplating the higher worlds.

When my father spoke to me about a betrothal to a rich girl with a large dowry, I did not care in the slightest. Except for one thing: I confirmed that her town was big enough to have a *bet midrash* that would be stocked with books of mystical wisdom for me to consult and study.

After the wedding, I moved in with my in-laws. They had pledged in the engagement contract to support me in my studies for two years, after which I was supposed to learn my father-in-law's business and earn a living as his partner.

But I did not care about business. The teachings I had uncovered showed me that this world is a veil of illusions, and that the worlds of truth are the higher emanations closer to the Holy One, Blessed be He, in all His Glory and Perfection and Infinity. And so, I spent all my time in the *bet midrash* studying the holy books of the *Kabbalah*, penetrating the mysteries of the *sefirot* and the roots of different souls.

The only obstacle to my complete happiness was my wife. On my wedding night, when I approached her bed, I knew what was expected of me to sire a Jewish child. My wife lay there in her flimsy nightgown, smiling and taunting me with her exposed flesh. Her bare legs were rubbing against each other, like an animal in heat.

I undressed and lay down next to her. But when I touched her cheek, it felt so cold and slimy that my hand recoiled. With much hesitation and dread, I tried touching other parts of her body—her thigh, her hand, her breast—but each time, it was the same revolting icy dampness. And the longer I lay there, the more I inhaled that nauseating hot breath from her mouth, which stank of burnt garlic.

When I could no longer bear this misery, I fled to the next room and buried my head in a pillow on a sofa.

I fell asleep to the sound of my wife weeping.

After that night, I avoided my wife. I would sleep on the benches in the *bet midrash* and not return home for days. My wife would visit me there and bring me food. She would adorn herself in all her finery—dresses that flattered her figure, glittering jewels, even alluring perfumes. The other men in the *bet midrash* would stop their studies and stare at her hungrily, clearly envying my beautiful bride. But I could not forget the cold slimy wetness of her skin, and when she came close, I swore I could smell a stale moisture—like a bog or a swamp—rising up from her flesh. I tried to avoid looking her in the eye, but when I did, I saw the great effort she made to conceal her sorrow and her shame.

Many months went by. People in town started to whisper about how my wife was not yet pregnant, and they blamed me for spending all my nights sleeping on the benches in the *bet midrash* instead of lying with my wife in her bed, the way a husband should. My in-laws and some of their relatives and even the town's rabbi pressed me to spend at least some of my nights at home so that I could do the things that a Jewish husband was supposed to do. Didn't I want a son of my own, they asked, a boy to whom I could teach the Torah and who would one day say *Kaddish* for my soul? How could I be so cruel and selfish as to deny my wife what was her due—a husband's loving embrace, and a cooing baby to nuzzle against her bosom?

On the one hand, I knew that I was obligated to perform my duties as a husband. Yet on the other hand, these concerns felt so puny, so trivial—such irritating little distractions from the higher truths of the universe. Our souls contain sparks of the light of the Holy One, Blessed be He, scattered during Creation and trapped now in this material world of illusions and husks. Our bodies are prisons that prevent our holy souls from ascending to higher worlds. To turn away from the sacred writings of the *Kabbalah* to embrace my wife's body would be to have my soul burrow itself deeper into this dungeon of flesh and bone. This was no doubt what I sensed when I touched her—how she reeked of the lowness, of the putrid corruption, of this material world.

Matters finally reached a head when the other scholars in the *bet midrash* forcibly expelled me from the building and denied me further access to my holy books. They said they had heard of the scandal of how my wife was not yet pregnant because I would not spend the night in my own home. I was a learned man, they pointed out, and so I knew exactly what duties a husband owes to his wife. I would not be permitted to study again until peace was restored in my marriage.

And so, I sighed and left the benches of the *bet midrash* to return to my in-laws' house. My wife looked at me so hopefully. I prayed to *HaShem* to fill me with the overpowering desire for a woman's body that I had read about other men feeling—that wild, pulsating carnal lust that the sages of blessed memory had so often warned against—but which I had never felt.

That night, I lay down again next to my wife. I rolled over and took her in my arms. She smiled at me—I had never seen such joy in her eyes. Even though I felt the cold damp on her skin again, I forced myself to continue. I kissed her mouth and she slid her tongue upon mine.

But that tongue tasted vile—as if my wife had relieved herself of her wastes out of that end instead of the other end. I jumped up, fell over the side of the bed, and vomited all over the rug on the floor. My wife screamed and ran away. I heard her muffled sobs and her father's indignant curses and promises to get a divorce out of me and every cent of the dowry repaid.

But I did not care about my father-in-law's money. And while my wife's tears wounded me, what could I do? Some power from the upper worlds was determined to prevent us from having a child.

I could no longer remain under my father-in-law's roof and I could not retreat back to the *bet midrash*. Nor could I return home to my parents—their anger and shame at my failure as a husband would have been too much for me to bear. I needed to get away, far away, to a place where I could focus my thoughts and prayers and thereby discover why I kept failing to be a proper Jewish husband.

I fled from my in-laws' house to the main road, followed that road out of the town, and then left the road to wander into the woods. The thick foliage over my head blocked the weak moonlight and I stumbled about blindly in the dark, tripping over branches, ripping my clothes, cutting and bruising my flesh.

When the sun finally rose again, I had no idea where I was. But then I heard the sounds of men singing. At first, I thought they were bandits who would cut my throat. However, I quickly realized that the voices were singing in Hebrew, and their songs were prayers of love and devotion for the Holy One, Blessed be He. I followed these sounds until I reached a clearing where I beheld four old Jews wrapped in prayer shawls and *tfillin*, fervently praying and swaying back and forth.

Yet these men were not like any Jewish householders that I had ever met before. They were so thin and withered that I could see their bones sticking out from under their skin. Their clothes were torn and tattered, and they were barefoot.

They fell silent when I approached.

I asked them who they were and why they were praying in such a remote place.

One of the old Jews stepped forward and said to me: We are seekers of the truth who wish to elevate our souls. We have come here to pray so that we may dwell far apart from the snares of this world of illusions and demons. To atone for our many sins both in this life and in the past incarnations of our souls, we mortify our flesh and fast from one *Shabbos* until the next. It is our hope that, when the Angel of Death in his holy mercy comes at last to cleave our souls from the prison of our bodies, the Heavenly Tribunal will judge us worthy to enter Paradise.

Until now, no other Jew has come upon us here in this forest. But you did—and that cannot be an accident. Who are you? How did you find this clearing?

I also felt I had been led to these men for some important, but hidden purpose, and so I told my whole shameful tale to them: How I had been so repulsed and sickened by my beautiful bride's flesh that I could not perform the duties of a husband. How I wished only to study the wisdom of the *Kabbalah*, but I was no longer permitted to enter the *bet midrash*. How I had fled and how my steps towards that clearing had been blind and aimless in the dark night.

The old Jew nodded as I spoke. When I finished, he said: Your steps were not at random. You were guided to this place. Your concentrated thoughts upon the esoteric, secret meanings of the Torah had caused the holy sparks buried deeply within your soul to stir and awaken. They yearn now to be free from their captivity in your body. They wish for you to atone for your sins so that your soul may enter Paradise. That is why you could not feel lust for your wife—her physical body is nothing but wretched ugliness to the divine light rousing inside you.

That day, I joined the spiritual brotherhood of these old men. To elevate my soul and atone for my many sins, both in this life and in past incarnations, I too fasted from one *Shabbos* to the next. On Friday evenings, we would travel to a nearby *shtetl* and beg charity from the Jews there. We would humble ourselves and conceal our learning and wisdom, so as not to be guilty of the sin of pride. And also, if we had revealed our true spiritual powers, the people there would have dragged us back into their petty affairs. We would then have been like you, Reb Israel ben Eliezer, Baal Shem Tov, demeaning our souls and our learning by selling amulets and cures and potions.

With this, the *dybbuk* stopped speaking and Ruth's mouth broke into a contemptuous smirk. Yehiel saw the Baal Shem Tov's face darken and grimace. But then his features relaxed and, in a gentle voice, he urged the *dybbuk* to continue his tale.

And so, the *dybbuk* spoke again: And I did not merely fast during the week. I also mortified my flesh. I tore branches from the trees and spent hours beating them against my skin. After a heavy snowfall one night, I tore off my clothes and rolled naked in the snowbanks, gleefully watching my fingers and toes turn blue.

And as I made war upon my body, I felt my soul drifting away into the crisp air above me. I heard the birds sing songs of praise and love for *HaShem*, and I joined in with them. I would close my eyes and sway in the breeze and behold visions of pink forests with golden paths that led to palaces of white marble vaulted high against the bright blue sky.

But when I knocked at the gates of those palaces, there was no answer. I could see men peering out of the windows above me, their faces glowing with holiness, but when they saw me looking up at them, they averted their gaze and fled inside their towers.

I asked my fellow *Hasidim*: What was I doing wrong? Why did I not merit entrance to the palaces of these holy men?

And they answered me: It is because your atonement is incomplete and you remain soiled with too many sins. You must strive harder to repent. Find what little pieces of pleasure you are still savoring in this lowly world of lies and crush them. Every moment must be devoted to repentance. For soon enough you will die, and then the merciless judgment of the Heavenly Tribunal shall be upon your soul.

I heeded their words. From then on, every time I felt my mind wander off with the slightest delight—the sound of a bird singing its song, the feeling of the sun warming my cheek, the pleasant smell of a flower—I would grab a stick to poke and stab at my sores and blisters until the pain was so unbearable that I would faint.

But no matter what I did, the gates of the palaces remained barred and the holy sages concealed their faces from me.

One night, when sleep evaded me, I went for a stroll to ease my restless nerves. Under the bright light of a full moon, I walked a little past the clearing until I suddenly came upon a well-tended footpath cutting through the forest. I was sure, though, that there had not been any such path there before. Could this mysterious path be a sign? Could an angel be leading me to a place where I could at last learn the secret to repairing my soul?

As I began to walk down this path, a blue light appeared before me, like a rock suspended in the air. I reached out, but it was just beyond my grasp. I followed this blue light as it led me down the path deeper into the woods. Soon the branches over my head grew so thick that they blocked the moon, and I could only see by the blue light hovering before me.

The path ended in front of the entrance to a cave. The blue light darted inside. At first, I was scared to follow. But with the moon hidden behind the high tree branches, the blackness of the night pressed down hard upon me and squeezed my chest. And so, I went into the cave to try to find the light.

Once I was inside, I saw the blue light again, bigger and brighter than before. It led me into a tunnel that twisted and turned and lurched downward for a long time until I came to a staircase descending further into the ground. When I reached the bottom of the stairs, the blue light disappeared and I found myself standing in a vast underground cavern lit by a dim orange glow. While the ceiling and the walls were shrouded in a distant darkness far beyond the point where I could see, the ground beneath my feet was a wide road made from white marble.

The cavern was completely silent.

Walking down this marble road, I beheld many buildings on either side of me, all fashioned from finely cut marble or grey stone blocks. I tried opening a couple of the doors, but they were bolted shut—even if I had the strength of an ox, they would not have budged.

I saw no one—that is, I saw no living person. But there were statues everywhere, all of which resembled men and women doing some normal everyday bit of business—buying food, arguing about something, scolding a child—but who had been frozen into marble.

I touched one or two of them; they were cold and hard.

I kept walking deeper and deeper into the underground city in the cavern. I cannot tell you for how long I walked, but it felt like many hours. Still, I was never weary and I never rested.

When I at last reached the end, an immense building rose up before me. I walked up its sloping, broad staircase until I reached the portico, which was decorated with thick round columns. There, I spied an open door and went inside.

I now found myself standing in a wide chamber lit by several torches placed in notches along the walls. In the center of the room there was a statue seated on a throne and an altar. And upon the altar, there was a goat tied down, writhing and making soft noises.

A man in a white robe suddenly appeared by my side. He was tall and distinguished, with a thick grey beard and lines on his forehead. Handing me a knife, he said: The one seated upon the throne can ease your suffering and repair your soul. Go to him, make the sacrificial offering, and seek his blessing.

I started to ask the man what this place was, but he vanished back into the air, leaving me alone with a knife in my hand. I walked up to the altar and looked closely at the statue. Below the neck, it appeared to be a man of mighty strength who wore a cloak made of animal skins.

But the head—how can I describe it? It had no face. There were ears and a chin and hair, and even wrinkles on the brow. Yet no eyes, no nose, and no mouth.

I was not sure what to do. To sacrifice the goat as an offering to an idol would be a grave sin, far more horrible than any sin I had ever committed before. But was this an idol? What kind of an idol had no face? That lack of a face—was that not a symbol of how the Holy One, Blessed be He, in His Infinity, has no human likeness?

I reminded myself that I had been led to this strange place by some power far greater than my puny, finite self. I thought: This must be a test to judge whether I was able to see beneath the surface illusions of the world—to see that what appeared to be a place of idolatry was actually a place of holiness. Perhaps I had been led to that very spot to redeem a spark of holiness trapped within this idol, and I needed to make the offering to elevate that spark back to the higher realms.

And so, wielding the knife in my hand, I swiftly cut the goat's windpipe in one clean stroke, in a proper kosher slaughter. I then offered up a prayer to the Holy One, Blessed be He, to repair my broken soul and lift it up to Paradise. Yet right after I spoke my prayer, the ground beneath me began to tremble and I fell to the floor. I tried to stand back up again, but a rock flew down from the ceiling and knocked me over. Then another rock fell upon my head, crushing my skull.

For a long time, everything was dark. And then I beheld the Angel of Death with his hundred eyes. He swung his long knife toward the navel of my corpse and suddenly my soul drifted free. I flew up, out of the cavern and into the forest, where it was now daylight under a bright and clear sky.

But something was wrong. The Angel of Death should have brought my soul to the Heavenly Tribunal to be tried and judged. What was I doing roaming about the forest again?

And then I suddenly felt a terrible burning pain, far worse than any pain I could have ever imagined when my soul was living in its bodily husk. I turned around and saw three tall, winged creatures in white robes. In their hands were whips made of fire, with which they were lashing my soul.

I pleaded with them to stop. I said that I had devoted my days to study and repentance, and to the repair of my soul. All I sought now was to be brought before the Heavenly Tribunal for judgment.

These beings—angels, demons, whatever they were—said nothing in response, but continued to strike me with their fiery lashes.

I fled, and they chased after me, pursuing me all over this world. Sometimes I would hide in a tree or a rock or an animal— and even once in a fish—but these vessels were not built to contain a human soul, and so they would eventually spit me back out.

After wandering in this way for many months, I came to this town. I heard the sounds of a girl weeping. It was the maiden Ruth, in whose body I am now resting, and she was sitting alone in her room with her hands and legs covered in blood.

I whispered into her ear: Why are you sad?

And she answered me: Today, for the first time, I started to bleed from my shameful parts, and it will not stop. I am soiled and disgusting and I cannot become clean again.

I replied: Do not fear. This lowly material world of blood and suffering and shame is but a brief passing illusion for your soul. It is not your soul that is shameful, but this body, into which your soul was cast down and imprisoned.

She then said: Who are you? Can you help me?

And I said: I am a wandering spirit. If you permit me to enter your body, I can help you.

The maiden Ruth then opened her mouth and I penetrated into her. Once our two souls were sharing the same body, I taught her the wisdom of the *kabbalah*, of how this world and these bodily husks—these heaps of stinking, sweating, bleeding flesh—are demonic illusions that conceal the true holy sparks trapped within our souls.

Reb Israel ben Eliezer, holy Baal Shem Tov, I have now answered your questions. You know who I am and what deeds I have done.

Ruth's body flopped back down on her pillow, and her glazed eyes seemed to Yehiel to be fixed on a point far away.

There was a thick, heavy silence throughout the synagogue.

Yehiel turned his gaze back to the Baal Shem Tov. The kabbalist had closed his eyes again and was swaying back and forth, mumbling something to himself, apparently oblivious to all the Jews mutely watching his every gesture. And then suddenly, he stood still, his eyes opened, and he extended his forefinger, shaking with rage, at Ruth's body.

He said: Foul spirit, vile *dybbuk*, you are a disgrace to the holy community of Israel. You shamed and humiliated your wife and then you ran off in the night like a thieving peasant in fear of a beating from his lord. While you say you entered the woods to repair and elevate your soul, in truth, you fell in with demons, who led you to their desolate city to make an offering to the idol of their false god.

The terrible punishments inflicted upon you so far are but a tiny fraction of what the Heavenly Tribunal has decreed in its harsh judgment upon your soul. But even these have failed to dissuade you from your evil path. For instead of meekly submitting to the just chastisements of the avenging angels, which serve as a penance for your many crimes, you have used your cunning to trick an innocent girl into letting you penetrate into her body. You know well, *dybbuk*, that the avenging angels with their whips of fire will not harm an innocent and righteous Jewish maiden, a girl destined to be a Jewish wife and a mother—a girl who may one day merit the blessing of seeing her grandsons or even great-grandsons called forth to read from the Torah before this very congregation.

Far from helping this maiden Ruth, you have sought to incline her heart toward your own depraved ways. You say that you have taught her to despise her body? You are stopping her from eating— you are starving her into an early grave, and you are making her scratch and tear at her own skin. The Holy One, Blessed be He, created the flesh of this girl to bear Jewish sons and suckle them at her breasts—to kiss their brows and nurse them with warm broth when they fall ill. Who are you to question His decree to create this girl's body and place her soul within it?

But it is not my task to pass judgment upon you, *dybbuk*. I am here to free the maiden Ruth from your captivity. I command you, now, by the power of the holy names that I have spoken today, to make your way to the little toe of her left foot and exit her body from the space between the nail and the skin.

When the Baal Shem Tov finished speaking, Yehiel turned his gaze back to Ruth. But her body did not stir and the *dybbuk* said nothing in response.

After several minutes passed in this silence, the Baal Shem Tov waved his hands again at his disciples. They raised the seven *shofroth* once more and blasted out several notes in unison that echoed loudly through the hushed synagogue. Another group of the Baal Shem Tov's disciples again used a candle to light their bowl of brownish powder and placed the scorching, putrid flames right beneath Ruth's nostrils.

Ruth's body coughed violently and shook and tried to turn away from the smoke, but a disciple who was not holding the bowl grabbed her head and forced her to inhale the fumes. Yehiel feared that his Ruth would not survive this torment—that she would suffocate—but then he reminded himself that the spirit must be driven away from her body. The Baal Shem Tov possessed the wisdom and learning to know how to expel a *dybbuk* and he did not.

At the same time that the putrid smoke was being forced into Ruth's nose, the Baal Shem Tov moved his mouth right next to her left ear and began rapidly intoning a series of Hebrew-sounding words that Yehiel did not understand.

And then the *dybbuk*'s voice cried out again from Ruth's mouth: Enough, mercy, please, Reb Israel Baal Shem, I will depart from this girl, as you command. I will depart through her little toe. But please, cease your torments.

The Baal Shem Tov then signaled to his disciples, and they moved away from Ruth and retreated into a corner.

The Baal Shem Tov spoke once more: *Dybbuk*, why should I trust that you will keep your word and not deceive me? Tell me by what signs I shall know that you have departed from this girl Ruth's body.

The *dybbuk* replied: When I leave her body, I shall fly out of this synagogue and break a hole in the window across from where the maiden Ruth's body now lies.

The Baal Shem Tov nodded at this suggestion, apparently satisfied. But then he asked another question: Tell me, *dybbuk*, what assurance do I have that you will not return again in the future to torment her?

The *dybbuk* answered: I fear the punishments that you will inflict upon me.

But the Baal Shem Tov said: You will fear the fiery lashes of the avenging angels more. I will instruct one of my disciples to say *kaddish* for your soul and to study a page of *Mishnah* each day in your honor. By means of these *mitzvot*, you will be protected from any angels or demons that may seek to do you harm. However, should you again attempt to haunt or possess this girl Ruth, I will withdraw this protection and summon the mightiest angels, with the sharpest whips, to pursue you without remorse. Do you understand? Are you agreed?

The *dybbuk* replied: I understand and I agree.

Then the Baal Shem Tov said: It is time, *dybbuk*. Depart at once and remember our pact.

Yehiel now turned his eyes to Ruth. Her expression struck him as sad and gloomy. He wondered if those were the emotions of the *dybbuk* or his daughter—could she be sorrowful that the spirit was about to depart? But no—the spirit was torturing her, twisting her reason and ravaging her body. It could only be the *dybbuk* who was sorrowful, as it did not want to be sent back to whatever desolate wastes it was cursed to wander.

Yehiel watched as Ruth's throat swelled as if she had swallowed a large rat. The growth then traveled down from her throat to her chest to her stomach to her thigh to her calf and into her left foot. There it paused, as if hesitating, before moving to the little toe of Ruth's left foot. With a loud pop, the nail burst from the toe and blood spurted out upon the bed. Ruth, in her own voice now, screamed in pain.

A moment later Yehiel heard the sound of glass breaking. He looked up and saw that there was now a hole in the window, just as the spirit had promised. His heart filled with joy: The spirit was gone and his Ruthele was healed. She would live, healthy and strong, and stand one day soon under the *chuppah* with her bridegroom. She would bear sons, many sons, and they would grow up to be fine Jews and mighty scholars of the Torah.

The Baal Shem Tov called upon Yehiel to rise from his seat and go to his daughter. Yehiel immediately obeyed, mounted the steps of the *bimah*, and sat down on the bed next to his Ruth.

Yehiel said to her: Do not worry, my *shayne punim*, you are cured now. The Holy One, Blessed be He, has wrought a great miracle today.

Then a few Jews approached the bed with a jug of milk, a loaf of bread, and a rind of hard cheese. Ruth grabbed the food and drink, rushed through the blessings, and devoured them right then and there in front of everyone. Cries of *mazel tov* went up all around her.

The Baal Shem Tov removed an amulet from his pocket and placed it around Ruth's neck. He told her never to remove it, as it protects against evil spirits and demons.

And then the Baal Shem Tov addressed the assembled Jewish householders of the town: Let what you have seen and heard today be a reminder to you and all Israel of the just and terrible punishment that awaits sinners in the next world, in the world of truth. Repent and atone now, while there is still time in this life, before your souls are judged.

At these words, many of the Jewish householders, perhaps thinking upon their own sins, turned pale and fell to the ground weeping and praying. But Yehiel could not think about anything other than how beautiful his Ruthele looked as she scarfed down her food.

IV. Matchmaking

ONCE THE *DYBBUK* had been driven out of her (and the Baal Shem Tov had received his ample fee and left town), Yehiel thought his Ruth seemed to be healthy again. While before she had refused to eat, now she was gleefully gluttonous, devouring honey cakes and *kugel* and *challah* bread faster than Malke could bake them. And while before she had sulked and spoken words full of contempt, now she smiled and hummed and played with her little brothers again. She helped her mother with the laundry and darned old clothes and linens. Yehiel even spied Ruth reading her Yiddish women's Bible, a sight that reassured him that the powers of the *sitra achra*, the other side, the realm of evil, had lost their grip on her soul and she was once more a pious and righteous daughter of Israel.

However, the exorcism had shaken the town. Having heard from the *dybbuk* of the punishments that awaited sinful souls, many Jewish householders repented for their sins, fasting, beating their chests, weeping and praying in the synagogue night and day, screaming out their terrible guilt and begging the forgiveness of *HaShem*.

But Yehiel could not bring himself to join in this frenzy of wailing, moaning atonement. He was simply too full of joy at seeing his daughter healthy and happy again. And so, he did his best to ignore the melancholy of his fellow Jews.

Unfortunately, Yehiel could not entirely ignore his fellow Jews, as he still had to pray in the same synagogue with them. There, the other Jewish householders appeared to Yehiel like wild, wandering spirits themselves: All that fasting and weeping had hollowed out their faces and left their eyes bloodshot and trembling.

Yehiel sensed that these emaciated men looked upon him now with disgust and scorn. Eventually, one Saturday morning, several of them grew bold enough to rebuke him publicly in the middle of the *Shabbat* service. Why, these men asked, was Yehiel not atoning for his many sins? Did he think that the commandments of the Torah did not apply to him? Did he not hear with his own ears what the *dybbuk* had said of the torments that await souls stained with sin?

But Yehiel replied: I shall fast and seek forgiveness of my sins during *Yom Kippur*, when all Israel gathers at the gates of repentance. For now, let me rejoice in the miracle of the return of my beloved daughter to good health. I suffered great torments when the *dybbuk* possessed her—that was punishment enough for my sins.

To which the householders responded: Fine, Reb Yehiel, you have suffered *your* punishment—or at least a portion of it. But what about your Ruth? How could an evil spirit have been able to penetrate into her unless she had committed some grave sin? The Holy One, Blessed be He, would not have permitted a *dybbuk* to possess the body of a girl who was truly pure and righteous. And did not the *dybbuk* himself say that she had willingly let him enter into her? How could that be unless she had wanted to transgress and do evil herself? And yet, Ruth has not repented. She whistles and sings and stuffs herself like some *goy*'s greedy pig.

At this point, the town's rabbi intervened. He rebuked the householders for slandering a righteous daughter of Israel. And, he continued, while *HaShem* welcomes acts of sincere repentance, an atonement that is exaggerated and flaunted before one's neighbors may be a sign of sinful pride and vanity, rather than humility and contrition. The Evil One has many snares to lure good Jews into error, not the least of which is to make a sin look like a *mitzvah*.

The rabbi's words doused the flames of excessive zeal in the town. The Jewish householders soon ceased their fasting and mortifications and returned to living as they had lived before. Nevertheless, Yehiel noticed that the other Jews now seemed to keep their distance from him, as if there were something impure or tainted about him and his family.

Ruth, though, seemed indifferent to the cold stares of her neighbors. In fact, she had almost nothing to do with these neighbors. She would spend her days alone doing her chores or studying her Yiddish Bible. When she ran errands—to buy something in the marketplace or to fetch water from a well—she did what she had to do as quickly as possible, sparing no time for idle conversation with the other women.

Exhausted by the burden of the harsh silent judgments of his fellow Jews, Yehiel resolved to leave on a business trip for several weeks. As a large shipment of timber was due to go upriver to the port of Danzig, Yehiel decided to travel on the barge with his Gentile laborers and use the journey as an opportunity to renew his contacts with the merchants in Danzig who bought his lumber. It had been too long, he mused, since he had looked them in the eye and reaffirmed the terms on which they dealt.

Yehiel enjoyed his time sailing up the river. Unlike his fellow Jewish householders, the *goyische* laborers navigating the barge did not rebuke Yehiel or slander his Ruth. Even though they had heard about the exorcism in the synagogue and plied him with questions about it, they were usually at least half-drunk when they raised the subject and mostly wanted to know what conjurations the Jewish exorcist had used. A couple of them had witnessed an exorcism performed by a monk on a Polish girl about Ruth's age who had been possessed by a demon. However, the monk had flailed about for three days trying to get the demon out of her, before the foul thing finally departed and left her alone. They were impressed with how quickly the Baal Shem Tov had driven the *dybbuk* away. The Gentile laborers debated amongst themselves whether the Jews had any useful techniques that the monks should be using. Some of them even said that the next time a Polish or Ukrainian girl was possessed, they should hire this *Zhyd* exorcist instead of calling upon the monk again.

Yehiel, for his part, reflected upon what he should do next. He could not continue living in a *shtetl* where the other Jews kept whispering slanders to each other about his Ruth. He would need to move somewhere new. The *Pan* who owned his *shtetl* and the outlying forests owned many other estates too. Yehiel could seek to acquire the leasehold rights to harvesting and selling the timber on these other estates. But this would take time. Any approach to His Lordship about such new opportunities must be made carefully, as the *Pan* would not want to risk losing Yehiel's payments on the current leasehold.

And a new business venture would complicate finding a bridegroom for Ruth. Prospective in-laws would wonder why Yehiel had left such a lucrative business as his current timber harvesting leasehold and if his new venture would succeed. They would hesitate to send their son into such an uncertain situation, even with a generous dowry. For this reason, it would be best to arrange Ruth's marriage before seeking out a new timber harvesting leasehold in another place. In fact, getting a son-in-law would help him establish the new business, as he would have another set of hands to help ease his labors.

With these thoughts running through his mind, Yehiel did not linger long in Danzig but quickly met with whom he needed to meet, transacted what business he needed to transact, and then returned home on a fast barge back down the river. When he had returned again to his *shtetl*, after an absence of a few weeks, he was pleased to see that all still appeared to be well with Ruth: She was now slightly plump, her clothes were neat and pressed, and her hair carefully brushed. All in all, Yehiel was more certain than ever that Ruth had made a complete recovery.

However, when Yehiel told Malke that he planned to visit the matchmaker, she begged her husband to reconsider as she was not so sure that Ruth was truly well again.

But look at her, Yehiel said, those rosy cheeks, that smile, that long thick hair? She is the picture of health. What could you think is still wrong with her?

Malke sighed and said: Yehiel, you think you understand but you do not. Girls are not like boys. When boys have friends, they study together or share a pinch of tobacco. But there are many parts of their souls that remain closed to each other—parts that are only shared between them and the Holy One, Blessed be He. Girls need friends to whom they can pour out the entire contents of their heart, with nothing left hidden. And these friends give each other counsel and comfort. Ruth once had such friends. But every time one of them comes around now to see her—and despite the evil gossip, they do, these old friends sometimes still seek to comfort her—Ruth sends them away. She may appear happy to her father but a girl of thirteen years old cannot be happy without a friend to whom she can secretly confide all of her loves and fears—all the things she cannot speak of to her *tate*.

But Yehiel replied: This is what worries you—that Ruth is not eager enough to make stupid idle chatter with silly girls? That she spends too much time attending to her chores and studying her Yiddish Bible? All the more reason she should get married, and without delay. The terrible ordeal she has suffered has made her wise beyond her years. She no longer has patience for childish things. If she now has the heart of a mother and not a child, then let her become a mother and give us grandsons.

Malke sighed again and her head fell down into her arms on the kitchen table. But Yehiel decided that he had already wasted too much time listening to his wife's nonsense. He was Ruth's father. It was *his* obligation to find a bridegroom, fix the dowry, and negotiate the betrothal terms.

Later that day, Yehiel sent word through the town's innkeeper that he was looking for the local matchmaker. The town buzzed with this news. Why the sudden rush to marry off Ruth? the gossips asked each other. Is her father worried that the *dybbuk* will come back and wants her wed to some poor sucker before that happens? Is he worried that there is some blemish upon her character—maybe the very blemish that had allowed the evil spirit to enter and possess her—and he wants a wedding before her secret is discovered?

But Yehiel ignored these slanders. As the matchmaker was just then away from the town, Yehiel decided to spend a couple of days back in the forest checking on his laborers and their progress in cutting down trees and sanding off the planks. He also visited the *Pan* in his manor house to pay an installment on the timber leasehold. While he was there, the nobleman and his steward detained Yehiel for a lengthy discussion of the timber market. The *Pan* strongly hinted that he had other estates that would be far more profitable if there were only a shrewd Jew like Yehiel to manage their forests and harvest their wood.

Shortly after Yehiel returned from the forest, the matchmaker came to Yehiel's house one night after evening prayers. This matchmaker was a man whom Yehiel had always loathed: loud, fat, with grease stains streaked all over his gabardine and the annoying habit of sticking his fingers into one's chest. But Yehiel needed to find a match for his Ruth, and this was the local matchmaker, and so he was forced to humor the man.

When the matchmaker entered Yehiel's kitchen, Malke and Ruth excused themselves so the men could speak privately. Once they were alone, the matchmaker began: Reb Yehiel, it is an honor and a pleasure to see you again. Your Ruth has grown up like a cedar of Lebanon, tall and strong. And so pretty! A fine daughter, *mazel tov* and many blessings to you. And now I am told you seek a bridegroom for her—wonderful! Tell me, what kind of a young man are you looking for? And what is the dowry, eh?

Yehiel smelled the damp sweat wafting from the matchmaker's armpits and felt again his longstanding revulsion for this creature. But he steeled himself and replied calmly: I seek a young man from a respectable home, although their lineage does not need to be the most esteemed. I do not need a mighty scholar, but a Jew with enough learning to run a kosher household and, most importantly, with a good head for business. Between us, my affairs have prospered greatly, may it happen to all Israel, and I will need a son-in-law who can become my business partner. I am willing to offer a substantial dowry—and then Yehiel named the number.

The matchmaker's eyes lit up like a chandelier when he heard the amount of the dowry. He spoke again: Reb Yehiel, you are a wise man, a shrewd man. Too many fathers come to me and want only the greatest Talmud prodigy—oh, and he must be descended from a long line of rabbis going straight back to Rashi of blessed memory. But then these same fathers find themselves saddled with a son-in-law who is a useless *luftmensch* good for nothing arguing about how big the jewels were on the breastplate of the High Priest in Jerusalem. You have the right idea—get a son-in-law with a nose for business. And with that dowry, they will be interested. But still, and I don't want to cast any aspersions on her honor, I am sure she is a wonderful girl, there was that matter of the *dybbuk*. Some people may be wary of marrying their son to a girl who was possessed—they will ask me what if the spirit comes back or attacks her bridegroom or their children? But I suppose if someone speaks that way, then their son was not the one destined for your lovely Ruth. I know some merchants, practical men, good Jews, who have sons who are the right age. Let me speak to them and see what I can arrange. *Baruch ha-Shem*, hopefully you will be a grandfather soon.

Shortly afterwards, the matchmaker left town again. He and Yehiel exchanged a flurry of letters over the next several weeks. As the matchmaker had warned, many bridegrooms were tempted by the large dowry, but wary of the *dybbuk*. Still, the matchmaker persisted and eventually wrote back with good news: He had found just the right young man. This bridegroom lived three towns over and his name was Nahum. His father leased a distillery from the local nobleman. The boy had a good head for business and wasn't looking for a father-in-law to support him in his studies. To the contrary, he wanted to start out in business right away as he had had enough of swaying over tractates of the Talmud. Nor was Nahum worried about the *dybbuk*: He told the matchmaker that should the spirit happen to come back, for whatever reason, he will simply pay some other *baal shem* to get rid of it again.

Yehiel was overjoyed and wrote back immediately to the matchmaker asking him to bring Nahum and his father over for a visit, so the boy could meet Ruth and they could make sure the couple was a good match.

About two weeks later, Nahum and his father arrived with the matchmaker. Even though the boy was only a couple of years older than Ruth, he already spoke like a seasoned merchant. Yehiel felt sure this Nahum would be perfect as his new business partner. He would teach him the timber trade, and then the two of them together could manage the leaseholds for the *Pan*'s forests scattered across his many estates.

With their fathers present, Nahum and Ruth met briefly. While they were clearly awkward with each other, Yehiel reminded himself that all young couples are awkward when they first meet. He and Malke had been no different. And regardless, Nahum pronounced himself quite pleased with the bride. He said that Ruth was a fine young lady and very pretty.

Nor did Ruth voice any complaints about Nahum, although, truth be told, she did not give him any compliments either. Ruth seemed, if anything, profoundly uninterested in discussing the topic of Nahum. But Yehiel chalked up her silence to a proper Jewish girl's modesty and bashfulness.

Feeling amply satisfied with this match, Yehiel commenced negotiations over the betrothal terms with Nahum's father. With the matchmaker as their go-between, they haggled with each other for the next few weeks over this or that detail. But soon enough, everything was arranged and agreed upon.

V. Drowning

IT WAS ON a Friday night, during *Shabbat* dinner, that Yehiel told Ruth the happy news: The betrothal terms had been set and she was to stand under the *chuppah*, a beautiful bride, in only a few months' time. Yehiel added that he looked forward soon to hearing the sound of his new grandson laughing in that very kitchen.

But when he looked across the table at Ruth, she was not smiling or blushing. She was staring at the ground, and Yehiel thought he even saw a tear tremble in the corner of her eye. Then Ruth quietly turned back to her food, laboriously eating the goose meat on her plate.

Yehiel was not sure what to do—he had assumed that his daughter would be happy—more than happy, overjoyed, excited—to become a bride. After all, what else did she expect to be? A righteous daughter of Israel grows up and she becomes a Jewish wife and mother. It was Yehiel's duty, as her father, to see that she was wed to a fine and upstanding bridegroom, a husband who would provide for her and her children and who wouldn't be some lout or drunk. And he had found just such a boy—Nahum had all the makings of a rich man on the rise, a magnate to be, who would one day buy her a grand manor house packed with servants at her beck and call. And he would hire the finest tailors to make dresses for

Ruth from the most expensive fabrics—dresses that would be the envy of the most refined Polish countess in Warsaw. *Nu*, what more could she want? What more was Yehiel supposed to have done for her?

Yehiel turned to Malke in the hope that perhaps she would speak in favor of the match. But she averted her gaze from his eyes. Even his little sons slinked away and left their honey cake untouched.

Yehiel decided to try again. He said: Ruth, don't you want to be a bride?

Without looking up, Ruth replied: Of course, *Tate*, I wish to be a bride.

Well then, what can be troubling you? Is Nahum not pleasing to you? You two seemed to get along fine when you met. He is a sharp boy, that Nahum, and he will be a shrewd merchant. You and your children will have everything you could desire—the finest delicacies, the loveliest clothes. What more could you want from a bridegroom?

Again without looking up from her plate, Ruth replied: Nahum is a fine young man and an excellent match, *Tate*. I cannot object to him.

Yehiel then pounded his fist down on the table and yelled back at his daughter: If you cannot find fault with your bridegroom, then why are you acting like a mourner at a funeral?

Ruth did not respond this time but burst into tears and ran off. Malke now turned to Yehiel and rebuked him: Why are you tormenting the poor girl? I told you she had not yet fully recovered her health, but you wouldn't listen, no, you had to go out and find her a match. A girl Ruth's age, what does she know of livelihoods and supporting children? You should have listened to me. You should have waited.

Bursting with fury, Yehiel said to his wife: You want us to wait around here, in this town, where Ruth is slandered every day? Where every Jew suspects her of some hidden, terrible sin that allowed the *dybbuk* to penetrate into her body? I found a fine bridegroom, from a good family, who could not care less about spirits and demons. With him, she can start anew. I will secure a new leasehold from the *Pan*, in one of his estates far from here, and I will send Nahum, with Ruth by his side, to settle in that distant place. And there they will be free from all these vicious lies.

But, Yehiel continued, we have not yet set a wedding date. That can be delayed a bit. We can perhaps put off the wedding for a year, until Ruth has had a chance to recover a bit more. Maybe she is scared of what will happen on her wedding night? Or she is scared of carrying a child in her belly? Perhaps, Malke, you can speak with her, to let her know how these things bring joy to one's home?

Malke nodded and reached for Yehiel's hands. She answered him in a calm, affectionate tone: Yes, let's put off the wedding for a little while. The groom is not going to fly away. Weddings are delayed all the time. These things take time. And I will speak to Ruth. Why don't you go to the *bet midrash*, have a glass of brandy, and study the weekly Torah portion? It will be easier for me to speak with Ruth about women's concerns without her *tate* here.

Yehiel agreed and left for the *bet midrash*. There, he sat alone on a bench in the corner, with a dim candle burning in the lamp, and tried to study. But his mind would not stay focused on the holy text. What did his Ruth want from him? Did she think kings and emperors were lining up to marry her? Did she not understand how hard it was to find a suitable young man who was not troubled at all by the fact that she had been possessed by an evil spirit?

Eventually, Yehiel looked around and realized that the other Jewish householders who had been studying there had left, and he and the gently snoring *shammes* were the only ones remaining. Yehiel sighed, stood up, and went back home. By the time he opened his door, the house was pitch dark and everyone was asleep. He went slowly up to his bed, reminding himself that Malke had spoken to

Ruth and no doubt eased whatever fears she had. And those fears were natural—he too had been nervous on his wedding day.

Yehiel spoke to Malke the next day. She told him that she had wiped away their daughter's tears and asked Ruth why she was not happy at the news that her *tate* had found her such a fine and righteous husband. Ruth responded that she could not bear the thought of a husband mounting her and sweating all over her, smearing her chest and face with his smelly drops of sweat; of a child growing inside her, wiggling around, kicking her, forcing her to think only about its selfish cravings; of the horrible pains of childbirth, the blood, the screaming; and of how the baby would feed on her as if she was a fat stupid cow, grabbing and biting and sucking at her breasts. Ruth cried out to her mother that this was too much misery—how could the Holy One, Blessed be He, inflict such suffering upon the daughters of Israel? What had they done to merit these punishments?

Malke told Ruth that these things were not as terrible as she feared. A husband's touch could bring a pleasure unimaginable until you felt it for the first time; there were remedies that the other women would teach her to help with pregnancy and childbirth; and Ruth could not understand the true wonder and beauty of the world that *HaShem* created until she looked into the wide, loving eyes of her own baby.

Did she heed your words? Yehiel asked.

Malke shrugged. And then she said: I am not sure. Let's give her some time. Just be patient.

Yehiel decided it was best to keep his distance for a while and not to pester Ruth about the betrothal. He visited the *Pan* again and received permission to tour the forests in another of His Lordship's estates, so that Yehiel could consider whether and how much to bid on the timber harvesting rights there. This trip kept him away for just over a week. And when he returned home, he immediately turned around and spent three further days away checking on his work crews in the nearby woods.

By the time he came back from this second trip, his household seemed to be at peace. Malke was smiling and humming and cooking; the little boys were playing some silly game with sticks; and Ruth was sitting in a corner, rosy-cheeked and healthy, mending some old clothes and gazing out with serene eyes. While no one spoke, this did not trouble Yehiel. After all, if he were to speak to Ruth, then he would, one way or another, wind up speaking of her engagement, and the two of them would trade harsh words again. Better to enjoy the quiet and let everyone's temper have a rest.

Later that night, Yehiel was awoken by a raging storm. The windows flashed wildly with lightning, and the panes rattled pitifully against the howling wind and hard pouring rain. The thunder boomed as if a hundred *shofroth* were being blasted all at once. His head pounding, Yehiel staggered from his bed downstairs to the kitchen pantry, where he found a bit of plum brandy to calm his nerves.

He wondered at how no one else in the house seemed to have been shaken from their slumbers. Had their ears lost the ability to hear? Or maybe there was no storm, and he had gone mad? But then another thunderclap reminded him that the storm was real. He sat down in a wooden chair, bleary eyed but awake, and sighed and drank the strong liquor until his weariness overcame him once more and he was able to resume sleeping in his bed.

However, because of that long stretch of sleeplessness, Yehiel woke up the next morning much later than usual and had to rush to get to the synagogue on time. After his morning prayers, he spent the next few hours at his warehouse checking the timber pieces marked for shipment to Danzig and reviewing his ledgers. When he was done there, he went to the river loading dock to confer with the captain of the barge about the freight fees for shipping his products.

Once he had settled his arrangements with the barge captain, he trudged slowly back to his house through the thick, viscous mud left by the previous night's rains. When he arrived back at his home, it was mid-afternoon and he found Malke in the kitchen, looking worried.

She rushed over to him, grabbed his arm, and asked if he had seen Ruth. Malke had not seen her all day, and she was not in the house or the marketplace. So, where could she be?

Yehiel replied that he also had not seen Ruth that day. Perhaps she had left for a stroll somewhere? Or maybe she had found a friend—didn't Malke keep saying that Ruth needed a friend? —and the two of them had gone off to do whatever girls that age do with their friends.

But Malke did not answer him. She hung her head down and sighed.

Yehiel then said he would go out and look for their Ruth. Malke squeezed his hand and thanked him.

And so, Yehiel grabbed his coat again, walked over to the marketplace, and asked if anyone had seen his daughter Ruth. But no one had. Then he tried the bathhouse and the *bet midrash* and the tavern, but again no one had seen her that day. He next looked in the women's section of the synagogue, but once more, there was no Ruth.

Growing concerned, Yehiel knocked on the door of every Jewish house in town, asking after his daughter, but to no avail. There soon formed a group of Jewish householders who took up the search with him, even asking the Ukrainians if anyone had seen Ruth.

As the sun was setting, they at last found a drunken peasant who said he had seen a girl by the riverbank. He offered to take them to her—for five zlotys. Yehiel cursed the bastard but paid him what he asked.

The peasant then led Yehiel and the other Jewish householders to a short, gnarled tree by the edge of the river. On the other side of it, in the water, he pointed to the body of a dead girl, with her long, wet hair tangled in the overhanging branches. But in the gloom of the twilight and the shadows cast by the tree, they could not make out who she was.

Two of the householders reached down into the water and hoisted the corpse up onto the riverbank. Then they dragged her over to where the light was still clear and gathered around to see who she was.

Yehiel fell to his knees and trembled, for he instantly recognized his Ruth. Somehow, madly, he felt that she would—that she must—stand back up, smile, and kiss her *tate* on the cheek. How could she be dead? She had been a healthy girl just last night, and now she was suddenly as stiff and lifeless as a wooden log in his warehouse? How could this be? It could not be.

A Jewish householder grabbed Yehiel by the shoulder and pulled him up. The man told Yehiel that the burial society had been sent for to clean the body and prepare it to be laid to rest. He should go home to his Malke to tell her the news before she heard it from somebody else.

Yehiel mutely obeyed, leaving the body to be watched over by the others. Several men accompanied him as he sluggishly walked home in a daze, each slow step forward full of pain. After a few steps, he remembered he should rend his garments and tore his gabardine slightly.

That night the burial society wrapped Ruth in a shroud and placed her body on the floor of Yehiel's kitchen, surrounded by candles. A kind old Jew, a tiny widower with almost no teeth left and a beard that resembled an overgrown dirty grey hedge, sat with her and recited Psalms all night to pray for Ruth's soul.

Malke screamed and wailed, as did the little boys, but Yehiel ignored them. He sat with the little old Jew reading Psalms, staring at the cold lump of his daughter's corpse and saying nothing. After gazing at her for a long time, he thought he saw a smile creep over her face, as if she were truly happy at last, as if all her cares had been lifted from her heart. Yehiel told himself that the Psalms must be working—that her soul was ascending to Paradise.

The funeral was a blur to Yehiel. *May the Lord of the Universe comfort you among the mourners of Zion and Jerusalem*—these words, spoken by one righteous Jew after another, seemed to reach him from somewhere far away, like a distant echo from a lofty mountaintop.

Yet there was one moment when Yehiel awoke from his stupor. After the coffin had been lowered into the ground, and the men from the burial society were busy filling the grave with dirt, a harsh wind suddenly blew against Yehiel's face, and he heard two voices laughing and squealing with delight. One was Ruth. The other he could not quite make out, although it sounded like a man's voice. But then the voices faded away, and he put them out of his mind.

VI. Mourning

THE NEXT WEEK, Yehiel sat *shiva* for his daughter. All the Jews in the town descended upon his home, offering their condolences, praying in his *minyan*, and bringing food. But their words of comfort left Yehiel with a bitter heart: These were the men and women, he recalled, who had whispered such vicious slanders about Ruth after the *dybbuk* was expelled from her, spreading cruel lies about how she must have committed some terrible sin for the spirit to have been able to penetrate into her. And now they had the *chutzpah* to act as if they were so grieved at the loss of such a pious and righteous daughter of Israel?

Yehiel was relieved when the seven days of mourning finally ended and all these hypocrites departed from his threshold. Yet then he was left alone with his brooding, unhappy thoughts. What had Ruth been doing in the river? Had she gone out the night before, in the midst of the storm? But why would she do a crazy thing like that? And what were those voices he had heard in the cemetery?

And there was another nagging thought that would not leave Yehiel in peace: Had Ruth wanted to die? She had suffered greatly when the *dybbuk* possessed her and afterwards she had been so alone. And despite her solitude, she still must have heard, one way or the other, of the vicious slanders being spread about her, even if she was too proud to acknowledge them.

He had tried to help her by finding a bridegroom, but that had only made her suffering worse. Had he attempted to force her to take a husband who was not pleasing in her eyes? But then again, how picky did she think she could be—after all, she had been possessed by an evil spirit.

Still, despite telling himself that he had acted rightly to secure a match with a fine bridegroom, and that there was no reason to believe she had killed herself, Yehiel felt he was somehow responsible for Ruth's death. That if only he had not pushed her engagement to Nahum so firmly—that if only he had offered her kinder words—more of a father's love—then maybe she would not have wandered out to the river and drowned.

It did not help that he felt the weight of Malke's silent judgment upon him. She spurned even the lightest touch from her husband, as if his fingers were made from burning sulfur that seared her flesh. She spoke to him now only about the most mundane matters—errands to run and the like—and in the polite but cold tone she would have used with a stranger on the street.

But Yehiel did not confront Malke, nor did he seek the intercession of the town rabbi to mend the fraying marriage. To the contrary, he felt that Malke's scorn was a just and fitting punishment for his many failures as a father.

Nor could Yehiel distract himself with his business affairs. The numbers in his account books seemed to jump up and dance before his eyes. He could not remember which logs had gone up the Vistula to the markets in Danzig, which were in his warehouse, or which were still sitting in the forest, freshly cut down. And when the steward of the *Pan*'s estate summoned him to consult about some matter or other, he pretended to be ill and unable to come.

He tried turning to study of the Talmud to ease his grief and restore clarity to his mind. But the words of the holy sages of blessed memory were just as scrambled and impenetrable as his account books.

With his embittered wife at home, and unable to focus on business or study, the one place left for Yehiel was the tavern on the outskirts of town. There, he would sit alone in a corner and linger with his glasses of vodka until he was sure that Malke had gone to sleep and he could return home without having to face her scorn. But then in the morning, with his head pounding, he would be filled with shame at his drunkenness the previous evening. And the weight of Malke's disgusted stares would rest even more heavily upon him.

Yet even the strong liquor could not stop the thoughts from swirling around in his mind. He remembered again the voices he had heard in the cemetery. One was Ruth. That made sense: Her soul was departing from her dead body. But the other voice he had not recognized, although it was certainly male. Could that have been the *dybbuk*, come back to torment them some more?

And then a new thought comforted Yehiel: If the *dybbuk* had indeed returned, then Ruth's death was not his fault. The evil spirit must have possessed her again and drowned her. Or maybe it had driven her so mad that she jumped into the river.

But how could the *dybbuk* have come back? After expelling it from Ruth's body, the Baal Shem Tov had provided two layers of protection against the wicked spirit's return. First, he had placed an amulet around Ruth's neck. Second, he had promised the spirit that, so long as it stayed away from her, his disciples would say *kaddish* for its soul and study a page of *Mishnah* each day in its honor and that by means of these intercessions the *dybbuk* would be protected from the fury of the avenging angels and demons.

Yehiel could not recall if Ruth had been wearing the amulet when they found her body in the river, as, in the shock of the moment, he had not had the presence of mind to check. And even if the amulet had not been around her neck then, the current of the river might have washed it away earlier—after all, who knew how long her corpse had been floating there.

If she had been wearing her amulet, and if the evil spirit had nevertheless still returned to torment her, then the only explanation was that the amulet was defective. Indeed, if the spirit had desired to return at all, it must have been because the Baal Shem Tov had not kept his word that his disciples would pray and study to protect the *dybbuk* from the flaming whips of the avenging angels. Yehiel had heard tales of other *dybbuks* that had been coaxed to depart from the living bodies they had possessed by a rabbi's promise to protect them with prayer and study, only for the rabbi to forget his promise later on, leading the *dybbuk* to return to its victim and exact a brutal revenge.

Putting his thoughts altogether, Yehiel concluded that the only way that the spirit could have returned was if the Baal Shem Tov had been negligent in his duties, either in writing the amulet, fulfilling his promises to protect the spirit, or both. It was the Baal Shem Tov who was responsible for Ruth's death.

But then again, Yehiel had to be careful. It was a great sin to make a false accusation, especially against a holy sage. Yet if it were the Baal Shem Tov's deeds, and not his own, that had driven his Ruth to an early grave, then he could be free of his guilt and his anguish. And he could reconcile with Malke.

Yehiel decided the only way he could learn what had truly happened would be to confront the Baal Shem Tov and demand an explanation for Ruth's death. And so, he sobered up, hired a carriage, and made preparations to travel to Mezhbizh, the *shtetl* where the Baal Shem Tov dwelt. He told no one where he was going or what he was doing, but rather just said vaguely he had to travel far away to meet with a merchant with whom he did business.

At sunrise on a clear and chilly Tuesday morning, he entered the carriage and the coachman drove off.

VII. Revealment and Concealment

AS SOON AS he arrived in Mezhbizh, Yehiel took a room in the local inn and asked directions to the house of Rabbi Israel ben Eliezer, the Baal Shem Tov. By the time he approached the house of the *tzaddik* on the outskirts of town, it was already late afternoon, and the street was deserted and silent.

He spied a tall thin Jew in an elegant gabardine standing on a porch and leaning against a railing. The man appeared lost in thought and did not seem to notice Yehiel.

Yehiel asked if this was the house where the Baal Shem Tov lived.

The man looked up now. He said that he was the scribe and secretary to the Baal Shem Tov and announced all visitors to the holy sage.

In response, Yehiel gave his name, town, and the name of his daughter.

The man did not say anything in reply, but quietly slipped away inside the house.

While he anxiously awaited the scribe's return, Yehiel reminded himself to be patient and stay composed—he had to learn the truth of what had happened to his Ruth. But then a new doubt arose in his mind: In his righteous anger, it had not occurred to him to figure out what, if anything, he wanted the Baal Shem Tov to do now. After all, Ruth was dead, and the dead will not rise again until the Messiah comes (may it be speedy and in our days). So, *nu*, what did Yehiel expect to get out of yelling at the holy *tzaddik*? Even if the Baal Shem Tov had failed to keep his promises, it did not matter anymore.

And yet, Yehiel could not turn back. At the very least, he wanted to know that his daughter was waiting for him to join her someday in the World to Come and that she was not a prisoner of the crazy *dybbuk* who might have trapped her soul who knows where. Yes, that was why he was demanding an audience with the *tzaddik*: to learn the truth and to ensure that his Ruth's soul was safe in Paradise, where she would be reunited with her parents someday.

The scribe eventually reappeared on the porch. Reb Yehiel, he said, while usually the *tzaddik* does not permit unexpected visitors to disturb his studies, he recalls how terribly your daughter suffered and thus he has agreed to see you now. He understands that you would not have traveled here unless your child was again in need of his aid.

Yehiel then followed him inside the house. They walked together down a dark hallway until they reached a study far in the back. The scribe ushered Yehiel into the room, withdrew, and closed the door behind him.

There, sitting next to a small writing desk, Yehiel recognized the Baal Shem Tov. Piled up around him were dense stacks of Hebrew manuscripts and slips of paper with bizarre Hebrew phrases written on them, perhaps to be used as amulets. Even though the sun was still bright in the sky, the Baal Shem Tov had closed the study's thick red curtains and the only light in the room came from two candles sitting on a table.

The Baal Shem Tov signaled to Yehiel to sit down in the opposite chair. Once Yehiel was seated, he leaned forward and asked what had brought Yehiel all the way to the threshold of his home in Mezhbizh—was Ruth in danger again?

The *tzaddik*'s eyes were full of worry and compassion.

Yehiel looked down at the ground and drew a deep breath. And then he said: Rabbi Israel ben Eliezer, Baal Shem Tov, holy *tzaddik*, thank you for seeing me immediately. You are right: I have come to you about my Ruth. After you expelled the *dybbuk* and departed from our town, our affairs progressed happily for a time. I even found her a bridegroom, a boy who was handsome, learned, and from a respectable family. But then one night, there was a terrible storm. The next day, a *goy* peasant found her dead body floating in the river. I could not understand how this had happened. What would my Ruth have been doing out of the house in the middle of a storm? And even if she were outside, why would she go to the riverbank? She never went there.

But later, when we buried her body in the cemetery, I heard two voices speaking in the wind. One was Ruth's voice. The other was a man's voice, although I could not make it out clearly. Still, I wondered, could it be the *dybbuk*? Had he returned? Did he kill her? But how could he have penetrated her body again when she had your amulet of protection? And why would the *dybbuk* even want to return to my daughter when your disciples were protecting it from the lashes of the avenging angels through their prayer and study?

And so, now I have come to you. Can you tell me how my Ruth died? Did the *dybbuk* come back? Was your amulet defective? Did your disciples fail to keep up with their studies and prayers? And where is Ruth now—is she with her grandmother of blessed memory in the World to Come, or is she trapped between worlds somewhere with that horrible spirit?

The Baal Shem Tov scratched his beard and sighed. And then he asked: Did you see the amulet on Ruth's corpse? Had she been wearing it the night she died?

Yehiel said that he did not know.

The Baal Shem Tov continued: I never give an amulet to a victim of *dybbuk* possession without checking it thoroughly, at least three times, for any blemish or mistake. And my disciples have prayed and studied for the spirit's protection every morning, just as I had promised. So, either the *dybbuk* did not return, in which case we need to understand how Ruth ended up in the river, or it did, and then we need to understand why Ruth ceased to protect herself with the amulet. And we are not going to learn the truth of these mysteries sitting here and speaking to each other. The answers are concealed in the next world, in the World to Come. I must prepare for my soul to ascend to the Heavenly Court. There, I shall ask the angels to reveal these matters to me. Are you staying at the inn?

Yehiel replied that he was.

Good, the Baal Shem Tov said, go back to the inn and wait there until I summon you again.

For the next two days Yehiel anxiously waited to hear from the Baal Shem Tov. Trying to feel hopeful for the state of her soul, he did his best to recall happy memories of Ruth: How she would sit on his lap when she was a little girl and pull on his beard and *payos*. Or when she would awake from bad dreams in the middle of the night and he would comfort her—those were not real, he would tell her, just silly things your soul makes up to play mean tricks on you when you sleep.

And then on the morning of the third day, before the sun was even up, the innkeeper roused him with an urgent summons from the Baal Shem Tov. After Yehiel quickly dressed and washed, he found the *tzaddik*'s scribe waiting for him in the doorway of the inn. They walked together in silence back to the Baal Shem Tov's house, where Yehiel was once more led into the same study in the back.

There, in the dim orange candlelight, Yehiel again beheld the Baal Shem Tov. But this time his eyes were bloodshot, his hands were trembling, and his clothes were smeared with what looked like long tracks of half-dried saliva. In a weak voice, the Baal Shem Tov asked for Yehiel to sit down and for his scribe to leave them.

Once Yehiel was seated, the Baal Shem Tov pulled out a flask, quickly mumbled a blessing, and took a long draught of something that smelled strong and bitter. With his nerves apparently fortified, the Baal Shem Tov now spoke more confidently:

I have found the soul of your Ruth, but it was no easy task. After I prayed with true, intense *kavanah* and invoked the appropriate combinations of secret names for the Holy One, Blessed be He, my soul lifted away from my body and ascended to the Heavenly Tribunal in the World to Come. Once I was there, I asked the angels in attendance upon the Throne of Glory to direct me to where I could find the soul of Ruth, daughter of Yehiel.

But they told me that there was no such soul in the World to Come.

How can this be? I asked them. The girl is dead and buried in the ground. Was her soul left lying in the dirt, trapped inside her rotting flesh? Had she been cursed to watch the maggots and worms writhe about her bones for all eternity?

Ask the Angel of Death, they replied. He will surely know the whereabouts of her soul.

And so, I invoked the special combinations of sacred names that compel the appearance of the Angel of Death. Soon he was standing before me, with his hundred eyes and long sharp knife.

He said to me: What do you want, little man? I should reap your soul this very instant as just recompense for daring to summon me.

But I was not afraid. I knew that the names I had recited were powerful enough to turn his knife to dust and to blind all of his one hundred eyes. Thus, I rebuked him: Quiet, angel, you do not frighten me. But as I know you have many important duties to attend to, I shall be brief. I seek the soul of Ruth, daughter of Yehiel. The angels of the Heavenly Tribunal say she is nowhere to be found in the World to Come. Where did you put her when you cleaved that soul from its body?

But the Angel of Death said: I have never reaped that soul.

At this point, I was losing my patience with all of these angels. The girl is dead and buried. Her soul must have gone somewhere. And whoever heard of a soul being forgotten by the Angel of Death?

So, I said back to the Angel of Death: Do you take me for a fool? The girl Ruth is lying in her grave and her heart has long stopped beating.

And then I quickly recited a slew of additional holy names. As soon as I was finished, daggers flew at those one hundred eyes. And the Angel of Death screamed in agony and begged me for mercy.

Heeding the cry for mercy, I ordered the avenging angels whom I had summoned to cease their torments.

The Angel of Death then spoke again: If a soul is so wicked and sinful that Ashmedai, King of the Demons, is certain that it will be condemned to suffer by the Heavenly Tribunal, he sometimes sends one of his demons to fetch it for him before I arrive. Ask Ashmedai about this soul—I am sure he has it somewhere.

I released the Angel of Death and permitted him to depart. Then I invoked the holy names that summon Ashmedai. And there he appeared before me, stinking of sulfur, with his goat legs and his horns, and scorpions crawling upon his skin.

I told him that I was seeking the soul of Ruth, daughter of Yehiel.

He replied that he did not recall that soul, but then again, there were so many souls in his realm, it could be difficult to keep track of them all. So Ashmedai summoned his demons and asked them one by one if they knew where Ruth was. But demon after demon, dozens of them, swore they had no idea what soul this was or where it could be. Finally, a little imp appeared who said that he knew where Ruth was, although the place was not in *Gehenna*. Ashmedai ordered the imp to take me to her and then excused himself, as he was needed elsewhere on pressing business.

The imp took me in his arms and we soared down from the World to Come back into this lowly material world. We flew over mountains and into a forest, and then through the trees until we came to the mouth of a cave. We entered the cave and descended into the damp, cold darkness until we reached a vast underground cavern illuminated by some kind of dim light, although I could not tell from whence the light came.

In that cavern, I beheld a wide paved road leading far off into the distance, and huge, elegant houses on either side of it. There were marble statues by the side of this road that appeared to be just like living people who had been suddenly frozen in place. Yet nothing was alive there—not even a buzzing fly or a blade of grass.

And then I remembered: This was the cursed place that the *dybbuk* had described, where he had committed the great sin of idolatry and met his death.

The imp carried me to a red marble palace. We went up the portico steps and through the open door, and then into a parlor room with a broad staircase leading to an upper floor. Up that staircase we went, then down a hallway, and at the end of the hallway, we entered a bedroom.

That bedroom was flooded with a bright light. I beheld a bed there covered with red silk sheets and red blankets. And upon this bed lay two souls—your Ruth and the *dybbuk*.

The imp loudly cleared his throat to get their attention.

The two souls recoiled in fear when they saw me.

I said to them: I have not come to harm you. I am here as an emissary on behalf of Ruth's father, who wishes to know how she died and whether her soul is safe. Will you tell me, Ruth, how you died and why your soul is resting in this desolate place and not in the World to Come?

And Ruth answered me: Rabbi Israel ben Eliezer, Baal Shem Tov, I am here with my *bashert*, my true bridegroom. My wicked father—those were her words—sought to bind me in chains to the lowly material world by marrying me to a greedy, conniving, filthy lout. I prayed for my true bridegroom—that beautiful spirit who had penetrated me and impregnated me with such visions of spiritual wonders—to come back to me.

And to ease the path of his return, I cast off your amulet and buried it deep in the ground.

I cried out to my beloved to come to me, to embrace me and to rescue me.

And then my bridegroom returned to me with the storm. As the thunder clapped and the lightning raged, he came back to me and asked me what I desired. I said that I wished to be with him and him alone, and to flee far away from the ugly, stinking world of these men of flesh.

My beloved said to me: Follow me to the river. And I did. Then he told me to lie down upon the water, and I did. Finally, he told me to let go of my body, to let it sink. And then I let my flesh drown and die.

Everything went dark. When I became conscious again, I realized I was lying in a coffin being lowered into the ground. I was terrified—where was he? Had he abandoned me? Had I been tricked into committing the sin of suicide by some cunning demon, so that I would now be tortured horribly in *Gehenna*?

But when I cried out again for my beloved, he came at once and cleaved my soul from my body. He whisked me away to this enchanted palace, where we shall live forever as true husband and wife, in spiritual bliss.

Listening to these words, I recalled how you treasured your daughter, Yehiel, and wished better for her soul than to be trapped between worlds in this cursed underground city. And so, I tried to appeal to her as a good Jewish daughter. I said: Ruth, your father is suffering terribly in his love and grief for you. How could you have abandoned him for this wicked spirit, the very same spirit that nearly starved and scratched you to death? Your father found you a fine bridegroom, a good Jew, with whom you could have had many sons. How can there be such cruelty in your heart? Don't you know that *HaShem* commanded you to honor your mother and your father?

But she scoffed and said: What you call starvation and suffering was the most sublime experience of pleasure and love. When my true bridegroom's spirit possessed my body, he showed me that the material world is but an illusion that conceals the sparks of holiness buried within our souls. He denied me food and mortified my flesh so that I could concentrate upon elevating my soul. But once you and my father and the rest drove my beloved away from me, I was trapped again, all alone, in that horrible body, a slave to its appetites and needs. That body even yearned to be touched in disgusting ways by the man whom my father had picked out to be my earthly groom. It craved for him to rub his rough, sweaty hide against it.

But these longings were snares and traps. What would have come from letting him touch me? Have your ears never heard the screams of women in childbirth? And have your eyes never seen the rags soaked in blood and urine that the midwives haul away after a baby is born? My body was a demon—it hungered to lead me astray into horrible pain and misery.

And then Ruth screamed at me and the imp to be gone and to leave her alone with her beloved, her *dybbuk*. Hearing such words from a daughter of Israel, my heart sank with despair and I lacked the strength to continue. My soul descended back to my body, and the vision ended.

And there is the truth of these matters, Reb Yehiel. You were cursed to have a daughter with a wicked soul. Be glad she departed this world as quickly as she did, before she could inflict even greater suffering upon the good, righteous Jews around her. Devote your remaining days to prayer and charity and good deeds, and you will have a fine portion in the World to Come. As for Ruth, think no more about her—her soul root was clearly putrid and rotten.

But now you must excuse me, as I need to rest. This long ascent of my soul has wearied me.

The Baal Shem Tov then stood up and left, leaving Yehiel alone in the *tzaddik*'s study. As he sat there in the stuffy room in the dim light, amidst the piles of half-finished amulets, he saw rising before him the long days of his life yet left to live, but he was no longer sure how he would muster the strength to endure them. He, too, felt the weight of his body now, and wished that his soul could depart and float away, and never be burdened again with such pain and sorrow.

Other Books by Barak Bassman

Elegy of the Minotaur

Repentance: A Tale of Demons in Old Jewish Poland

King Solomon and Ashmedai: A Wisdom Tale

The Twilight of the Magical Siren: A Tale of Late Antiquity

The Leper Princess and The Court Jew

The Last Confession of Joseph della Reina

The Gifts of the Fairy Melusine

Necromancy of the Demon Maiden: A Gothic Tale of Podolia

The Death of the Wizard Merlin

The Vampire and The Wandering Jew

The Emissary from Mezeritch: A Dark Hasidic Tale

The Beheading Game: An Arthurian Tale

The Holy Sinner: A Gothic Tale of the Baal Shem Tov

The Abduction of Queen Guinevere

The Cruelty of the Fisher King: A Tale of Perceval and the Holy Grail

The Baal Shem Tov and the Heretic: A Sabbatean Tale